Restoring *Hope*

PHILIPPA CLEALL

Ark House Press
arkhousepress.com

Cataloguing in Publication Data:
Title: Restoring Hope
ISBN: 978-1-7642813-3-1 (pbk) 978-1-7643577-8-4 (ebk)
Subjects: FIC042040 FICTION / Christian / Romance / General; FIC066000 FICTION / Small Town & Rural; FAM001030 FAMILY & RELATIONSHIPS / Abuse / Domestic Partner Abuse

Design by initiateagency.com

DEDICATION

*To my daughter, whose prodigal journey has led
her back into the arms of grace.*

CONTENTS

SCRIPTURE EPIGRAPH

"The Lord is close to the brokenhearted and
saves those who are crushed in spirit."
Psalm 34:18 (NIV)

AUTHOR'S NOTE

Dear Reader,

This story is fictional, but it has been shaped by real experiences. Both my own, and those of others who have walked through broken trust and difficult relationships with courage and faith.

Though *Restoring Hope* is not autobiographical, it was written from a place of deep personal understanding. My own journey has involved wrestling with forgiveness, safety, and the longing to honour God when the road ahead felt painful and unclear.

This novel explores some of those tensions: between hope and boundaries, grace and wisdom, faith and uncertainty, forgiveness and trust. The restoration Hope experiences is completely imagined, but I pray it points to what is possible when people are cared for with compassion, spiritual discernment, and moral integrity.

Restoring Hope was also written with a wider purpose: to open conversations within communities and churches about how we can better recognise and respond to domestic violence and coercive control. It is my hope that this story will help bring awareness to the often-hidden struggles faced by those in harmful relationships around us and offer a gentle invitation toward change, both personal and communal.

Whether you have lived through something similar, are walking along-side someone who has, or are encountering these themes for the first time, I hope this story offers comfort, insight, and courage. May it gently remind you that God not only heals wounds, but also defends the truth, shows mercy and justice, and draws near to the broken-hearted.

Thank you for stepping into this story. May it meet you where you are.

With grace and care
Philippa

A NOTE ON SELF-CARE

While *Restoring Hope* is ultimately a story of healing and redemption, it touches on themes such as domestic violence, unplanned pregnancy, anxiety, church trauma, and grief.

If you have lived experience with any of these, please be gentle with yourself as you read. It's okay to pause, to step away, or to seek support. You are not alone, and it can be helpful to reach out to a wise and trusted friend, professional counsellor, trained pastoral caregiver, or a relevant support organisation in your region.

Stories can stir deep places in us. May this one lead not to despair, but toward hope, healing, and the reminder that your well-being matters deeply. If you are part of a church or faith community, may it also prompt reflection on how we can grow in compassion and wisdom as we walk with others through complex and painful seasons of life.

CHAPTER 1

*W*oodsmoke hung in the morning air like a memory as Hope Elkins passed the newly restored *Hearth Café*, now open for business, and walked toward the road to set out her sign. Behind her, the last batch of par-baked pizza bases were finishing in the outdoor wood-fired oven, ready for toppings and a quick reheat once the orders began. The scent of crisping dough and olive oil drifted across the old bridge and down into Wombat Valley's main street.

Hope exhaled slowly, taking in the gentle warmth of this first day of autumn. After six months of quiet labour, which included installing a new commercial kitchen, overseeing the brick oven's construction, and sanding timber walls until her arms ached, the café was finally ready. It seemed longer than half a year since she'd walked away from city life and from a marriage that had splintered more than just her peace.

Her summer-lightened hair was twisted into a loose topknot, which she adjusted with fingers still carrying the faint scent of rosemary from the morning prep. The plain canvas apron she wore, embroidered with the café's logo, hid the flour streaks well. She brushed it absently, then stepped back to take in the building, admiring its freshly painted windows and railings, timber cladding, and wide verandah. This was what she'd built from the bones of grief. A space to begin again, not by forgetting, but by feeding into something new.

It had been a risk, pouring her inheritance into this project. But the valley, and her childhood memories of being here, had once held joy. Her grandmother had spent over fifty years living in Wombat Valley, baking and welcoming neighbours with open arms. Hope wanted that again. A place of warmth and nourishment. Something she could grow with her own hands.

The old cottage at the rear of the property, where she now lived alone with her tabby cat, Tiger, was too quiet. Loyal and a good listener, Tiger kept her company, but Hope missed the conversations she remembered from childhood visits. She could still hear her grandmother's stories, through the song of the kettle, as neighbours drifted in like family. She missed being around good people.

Taking a deep breath, she focused on being calm and steady. Today was reopening day. The dream she'd rebuilt from sorrow was about to begin. Hope went up the front steps and walked in.

Soon, the bell jingled above the café door.

"You've certainly brought this old place back to life," said Edith Alden, stepping inside wearing a felt hat over her short silver hair. Her sharp hazel eyes missed nothing. "You always were good with dough and people."

Hope's nerves hummed under her ribs. "Edith," she said warmly. "I wasn't sure if anyone would come."

"Oh, nonsense. Half the town's been waiting months for you to open. The other half are just slow walkers." Edith's eyes twinkled. "Even Joe Butler might be tempted to drop in and have someone feed him. That poor man's been working around the clock since losing his wife."

Hope smiled, touched by the familiar blunt affection. Edith had been one of her mother's closest friends, and a quiet pillar during the café's refurbishment. She often appeared with a warm meal at the end of the day, sensing when Hope hadn't eaten or slept properly. Now retired from the family dairy farm, Edith and her husband Rob had given the reins over to their son Craig. Edith's presence was a reminder of her childhood. She represented warm memories that stayed, even when everything else had fallen apart. With free time on her hands now, Edith was focused on hobbies like making jam and preserves and keeping an eye out for those in town who needed some extra care.

She took a seat in the corner, her presence like a lighthouse.

Soon, more people filtered in: Hanna the florist, two kayaking instructors in worn sunhats, a trio of Edith's friends from nearby farms, and a young mother with a restless toddler.

The toddler knocked over a plastic cup, juice spilled across the table. The mother looked stricken, close to tears. Hope crossed the room with a cloth and a calm smile.

"You're doing great, by the way," she said gently, offering a fresh cup. "Bringing little ones to a café is not for the faint of heart."

The mother blinked. Then gave a fragile, grateful smile.

Hope moved between counter and oven, the routine of café work a rhythm she knew well from city life. The cafes before had been sleek inner-city places with polished tiles, and city investors watching every margin. But this one was hers, to start at her own pace, as part of the long journey to healing.

Before long, the lunch rush softened. The café hummed with quiet conversation and clinking cutlery. A breeze stirred through the open front doors.

From a table near the window, she heard the low murmur of two older women.

"She's done it up beautifully," said one. "Looks like somewhere you'd take visitors to impress them, but you can still relax here with friends."

Hope pretended not to hear, but the words warmed her more than she'd expected. This was what she'd wanted to create.

Just as the café emptied of lunch customers, the front door jingled again. A tall man, lean but muscled, stepped inside. His wavy dark hair a little windblown. Behind him at the door sat a large scruffy dog.

"Hope?" he said, voice low and even.

She looked up into his coffee-coloured eyes and recognised him. Joe Butler. That voice, steady and deep, was unfamiliar. Disarming. The kind she wasn't sure she trusted.

"You're the vet, right?"

"Guilty." He gave a quick nod, eyes flicking briefly to the floor before meeting hers again.

For a second, barely that, he forgot why he'd come. She was just a woman behind a counter, yet something about her stilled him. Slender. Watchful. Eyes the colour of the sky before rain, shadowed by tiredness.

But somehow he couldn't look away.

That surprised him most.

He recovered quickly. "Came to see what all the fuss was about. Also …" He nodded back at the dog. "Picked up this stray from the farm next door. Might've twisted her paw chasing kangaroos this morning. Mind if we sit out back while I check her over?"

She hesitated, long enough for him to notice.

Joe's smile dimmed. "Sorry. That was presumptuous. I can stay out front—"

"Out the back's fine," she said walking forward, and opening the door to gesture around the side. "There's shade there. Water bowls too." She reached for something hospitable to say. "Since you're doctoring the wounded, I'll bring something out to keep you going."

Joe smiled as he passed her, his sleeve brushing her arm. She flinched. A tightening in her shoulders she couldn't quite suppress.

Joe didn't comment. If he noticed, he gave her the dignity of silence. That, somehow, felt like kindness.

***

Joe was sitting under the mulberry tree on the grass, examining the dog's paw, when Hope brought out a plate of margherita slices a few minutes later. His movements were slow and gentle, his voice a quiet murmur.

She stayed on her feet for a few moments, unsure whether to linger. But the quiet in the courtyard pulled at her, so she perched nearby, not quite settling.

Her eyes caught the flash of silver on his left hand. A wedding band. Still wearing it. She looked away, uncomfortable with how much she'd noticed.

"This girl's not limping badly," he said. "Just overdid it. Like most of us, chasing something too hard."

Hope raised a brow. "You mean like opening a café when half your life's still in boxes?"

He chuckled. "I meant me. Working every hour to keep the vet practice afloat while searching for a new partner. But, it sounds like, maybe you are too."

She caught herself smiling. When was the last time she'd felt so unguarded near a man?

They sat in quiet companionship, sunlight filtering through the tree. The dog rested at their feet. Brave little wrens darted around the courtyard, pecking at seeds between the bricks.

"You've done something special here," Joe said. "It feels … safe."

Hope looked around the courtyard: its stone walls, fruit trees, tangled jasmine over the arch, circular firepit, and blanket of grass leading to wild-flower garden beds. It was everything she'd pictured. She had thought safety would be found in solitude, but now realised she'd built something meant to be shared … and she would have to find a way to adjust to that.

"Thanks," she said quietly. "It's encouraging to hear."

From inside, the café bell jingled again. Hope stood, a feeling of discomfort rising at being alone with him for too long.

"I should get back."

Joe nodded, standing too. "If you ever need help with animals, taste testing, or anything else … I'm around."

She gave a small, cautious smile. "Noted."

As she stepped through the café back door, something unfamiliar rose in her chest. Not wariness. Something lighter. A flicker of warmth.

A few moments later, at the kitchen window, she spotted Joe feeding the dog pizza crusts while chatting on his mobile phone. The two of them were framed in her view by overhanging jasmine. The feeling stirred again. She hadn't planned to feel anything today other than nerves, and maybe relief.

But what settled in her chest wasn't either of those things.

It was awareness, and the uneasy pull of a kindness she hadn't asked for. And wasn't sure she trusted.

CHAPTER 2

The last of the café dishes clinked into the drying rack as dusk turned the Wombat Valley hills lavender.

Hope stood at the sink, hands resting on the edge. Her shoulders ached with that clean, honest fatigue that came from work, not fear. There was no tension, no waiting for someone's temper to turn. Just a café opening she was proud of. The day had gone better than she dared believe it would. But as the shadows stretched and the café emptied of warmth, so did the lightness in her chest.

Hope turned off the last light, double-checked the oven was cold, and stepped through the back gate toward her small cottage, tucked behind the rear courtyard. A lemon tree brushed her shoulder as she passed, and she caught a whiff of jasmine. Scents she used to love. Back before they began to remind her of other nights. Other kitchens.

The door creaked open and closed behind her. Silence. Then a soft meow.

Tiger stretched, his striped body arching as he wove around her legs.

"Okay," she said affectionately, reaching for a tin. "You've earned dinner too."

She fed him, then looked around the cottage. It was tidy, but sparse. Half her boxes still sat unopened, sealed like memories she wasn't ready to unpack. She'd thrown herself into the café refurbishment from day one, anything to avoid the stillness of being in the cottage. It echoed—grief, pain, and her own disappointment. The silence wasn't restful. It pulled at old memories like threads. And she wasn't ready to unravel them.

Her neglected journal had lain on her bedside table, untouched for weeks. She wrapped a throw blanket tightly around herself as she sat on the edge of the bed. The ache in her chest returned. She picked up the journal, stopping on a page dated four months ago:

> *"Lord, I want to believe You're still here. But everything feels hollow. My prayers feel like they hit the ceiling and fall back unheard. Where were you when I needed you?"*

Hope snapped the journal shut and rubbed her eyes. No wonder she hadn't opened it in weeks.

The ache stayed with her, low and familiar, as she brushed out her long wavy hair. The brush caught on a tangle, and she winced. Then a knock came at the door.

She opened it to find Edith holding a steaming mug of herbal tea and a thermos.

"Chamomile and honey," Edith said, lifting the cup. "For unwinding. Figured you might need it."

Hope hesitated before opening the door wider.

"Do you … just wander around with cups of tea at night?"

Edith grinned. "Only for my favourite neighbours."

Hope took the mug. Its warmth grounded her.

"Thanks. It was a good day."

"You fooled most of the town into thinking you were born for this," Edith said, settling onto the weathered bench just outside the door. "But I know that look, Hope. You're worn thin. You're only thirty-five, but your eyes—those beautiful eyes of yours that shift from blue to grey depending on your mood—they're carrying too much these days. The light's still there, but so is the weight."

Hope hesitated, then joined her on the bench.

"I thought I'd feel better today. Proud. Relieved. But now it's quiet, and I just … I don't know." Hope shook her head. "It all rushes back in the stillness. Things I don't want to remember."

Edith's eyes softened. "You didn't just leave a man behind when you came back to Wombat Valley. You left a life. And parts of yourself you're still trying to find." She paused, her voice quieter now. "You've been grieving a long time, love. Your mum died only four years ago. Your dad when you were still a girl. That's a lot of sorrow to carry."

Hope looked down into her mug. The tea smelled like her grandmother's garden. Safe.

"I used to think grief had a time limit," she said quietly. "Like after a year or two, the sharp bits were meant to dull. But sometimes it still sneaks up on me. I'll hear a song Mum loved, or see a father holding his daughter's hand, and it just …" She pressed her lips together, shaking her head.

Edith didn't speak. She didn't need to.

Hope let out a slow breath. "I think I stopped expecting good things after Mum died. And after Mark … I stopped expecting safe things too."

After a pause, she murmured, "I'm good at pretending. But when the lights go out …"

Her voice caught. She looked away.

"… the memories become loud," Edith finished.

The wind rustled the gum trees. For a moment, neither of them spoke.

"I used to believe God protected people like me. Girls who tried to do the right thing. Who waited for a good man. Who prayed before saying yes."

Edith reached over and took Hope's hand.

"I don't think God promises we won't get hurt," she said. "I think He promises we won't be alone in it."

Hope's voice cracked. "So, where was He?"

Edith didn't flinch. She put her arm around Hope.

"With you. When you walked out. In the quiet that followed." She nodded out towards the café, "In this."

She paused, then Edith added, gently, "You know you don't have to have all the answers before you start praying again."

Hope swallowed. "I'm not sure He wants to hear from me."

"Oh, darling." Edith's voice softened. She rested a weathered hand on Hope's arm. "He never stopped wanting to."

Hope swallowed hard, then nodded. A tightness eased in her chest. She wasn't ready to pray aloud, but something shifted. A small, silent whisper inside her heart:

"Are You still there?"

And in the quiet, a word formed in her mind. It felt like … the answer might be *yes.*

Tiger had been doing a figure of eight between their legs, but finally hopped up beside them, curling into a ball on Edith's lap with a satisfied purr. She scratched behind his ears.

"Wise cat," she said. "Knows good company when he finds it."

Edith reminded herself that true wisdom was knowing when to speak, and when to simply wait. Some truths are only safe to mention when the heart is ready to listen.

Edith began chatting about the café. "Ruth and Anne loved everything today: the pizza, the cake, and especially the coffee." She rolled her eyes affectionately. "They also love a good gossip, so you can bet the whole valley will have heard about your café by the morning. Brace yourself for a full house tomorrow."

Hope smiled. "I might need to find someone to help soon. A second pair of hands."

Edith mentioned that a local teen, Ruby, had been out to their farm last week asking if they needed an extra hand with milking. They didn't. Craig had Bob's grandson coming over most mornings to help.

Hope tried to picture Ruby's face. "I don't think I've met her," she said.

"She's rail thin. Long dark hair, freckles. She's actually a pretty thing but looks wary. Like a girl always ready to run."

Hope raised an eyebrow.

Edith's tone gentled. "Her home life hasn't been easy. She's taken off with a few different young men over the years. But maybe she's thinking about staying put now. Looking for local work could be a good sign."

Hope let Edith's chatter and encouragement wash over her like sunlight after rain. She smiled as Edith entertained her with stories about Rob's latest attempts to sneak back to work on the farm whenever Craig wasn't watching.

By the time the thermos was empty, Hope felt drowsy and peaceful.

After saying goodnight, Hope stepped into the quiet cottage, took a long, hot shower, and slipped beneath the sheets.

And for the first time in a long while, sleep came easily. Without fear.

CHAPTER 3

The late afternoon autumn sun spilled like honey across the hills of Wombat Valley. Hope wiped her hands on a tea towel, careful not to mark her new apron with tomato stains. The scent of distant woodsmoke curled through the air. Her cottage fireplace was finally working again after weeks of battling a blocked chimney.

She stepped out of the café's back door, stretching her arms above her head, then strolled toward her cottage to check the washing on the line. Beyond the sagging back fence, Bob Huxley's apple orchard glowed with rays from the setting sun. Its gnarled trees, lush grass, and fruit-heavy branches were just as she remembered from childhood visits to her grandmother.

Then, she heard a rustle in the still evening air.

Hope paused.

Through the branches, she caught a flash of movement. Someone was crouched low, with a dark hoodie, and quick hands tugging apples from a tree. Hope squinted. A young woman, or girl? Slender, wiry, and a defiant set to her jaw that looked like someone who'd been hungry too long to ask politely. Her backpack was slung low and already bulging.

"You alright out there?" Hope called, voice light but steady.

The girl jolted like she'd been shocked, eyes wide beneath the hood. An apple slipped from her fingers and rolled towards the fence. For a second, Hope thought she'd run. She looked like she might.

"I'm not going to call anyone," Hope added, stepping slowly into view. "You just startled me."

The girl didn't move, but her eyes darted around like a cornered animal gauging whether it could clear the fence.

Hope crouched, picked up the apple, and tossed it underhand. "Might as well take the good ones."

The girl caught it with a fumble. Didn't thank her. Just stood there, half-turned like she might bolt.

"You're Ruby, aren't you?" Hope asked.

The girl stiffened.

"Small town. Word gets around. You've been next door asking for work at Edith and Rob's place?"

Ruby said nothing, her jaw clenched.

Hope hesitated. The girl could steal more than apples. There was something in her posture, tight and coiled, that reminded Hope of herself not long ago. Trying not to look like someone who needed help.

Hope glanced back at the café. "I've got a dinner crowd coming in tonight, and no one to help me keep up with the dishes. You any good with scrubbing plates or using a mop?"

Ruby blinked. "What?"

"I need help. You look like you could use a job. It seems like something we could help each other with."

Ruby scoffed, folding her arms tightly across her chest. "You're offering me work after you catch me?"

Hope shrugged. "Apples fall off trees. People get hungry. You're not the first."

There was a beat of silence. A kookaburra laughed somewhere up in the gums.

"I'm not some charity case," Ruby muttered. The words were hard, but her posture said otherwise.

"It's not charity. It's work. Pay's nothing glamorous, but there's pizza at the end of it, and no one yelling at you. What do you reckon?"

Ruby's gaze narrowed, suspicious. But something flickered behind it. Hunger. Weariness. A tiny fracture in the wall. Hope could see the quiet calculations of someone who'd learned not to trust kindness too quickly.

Finally, Ruby nodded and tucked the apple into her backpack. "Just for tonight."

Hope smiled gently without pressure. "Okay."

***

Later, while Ruby had a shower and changed into some clean clothes Hope had dug out for her, Joe arrived at the back door of the café. The stray dog, now looking brushed and tidy, was faithfully beside him.

Joe shrugged. "There's no microchip, and no one's claimed her. That's unusual for an Aussie Shepherd. They're valuable and loyal."

Hope realised where this might be going and said, "I can't really keep her at my cottage, as I'm usually over here. She'll probably escape and wander off."

"She's already made herself at home here," Joe said. "And she likes your pizza scraps, by the way. So, I'd say she'll be keen to stay right here with you, keeping people company and an eye out for any food on offer. When we were last here, she licked the plate clean."

Hope raised an eyebrow. "This is all part of your grand plan to leave a dog on my doorstep, isn't it?"

Joe gave a sheepish grin. "Caught me. I'm hopeless at saying no to strays, four-legged or otherwise. And, I do have a habit of matching them up with good owners."

The dog wagged her tail happily, tongue lolling.

Hope sighed, but a smile tugged at her mouth. "Alright. Trial run. But just so you know, I'm not great with surprise visits from men. Or with advice I haven't sought."

Joe's smile faded. "I hear you. I can step back. I'll only offer help if you ask for it."

Hope stiffened, the old urge to protect herself rising like a shield. But when she looked at Joe, there was no trace of mocking or judgement, only quiet understanding.

"Healing takes time," Joe said gently. "That's something I've come to learn. But even in the ruins … peace can begin to grow. Especially when life slows down enough for you to hear your own voice again."

Hope was about to shrug it off, maybe make a joke, deflect the moment.

But something in his tone and stillness made her stop.

Hope looked away. Then turned back. She wanted him to understand.

"It wasn't physical violence," she said quietly. "Not in the way people expect. But he … controlled everything. Constantly put me down."

Her voice flattened. "He wanted to make me feel small."

Joe stayed still, hands in his pockets.

He didn't interrupt. Didn't try to smooth it over.

"I told myself it didn't count because there were no bruises," she added. Her throat tightened. "But I walked on eggshells every day. Like I was the problem."

She hadn't planned to say that. But the words had slipped out, like something that had been waiting for its moment.

The dog sat between them now, tail sweeping slowly across the brick pavers.

"I still flinch sometimes," Hope whispered.

Joe knelt, resting a hand gently on the dog's back.

"That kind of fear doesn't vanish overnight," he said. "It leaves a deep scar. One that keeps getting bumped."

Hope met his eyes, reluctantly. She didn't see pity. Just quiet knowing.

"Healing takes time," he added. "And trust … that's earned. No rush."

She nodded, swallowing the emotion in her throat.

Joe rose, brushing dog hair from his jeans. "I'll leave you to it. Just call if you need anything. Dog-related or otherwise."

He paused, then gave her a small salute. "Or tell me to shove off. That works too."

Hope laughed unexpectedly, a small puff of air through her nose. She sighed with relief. "Thanks. I'll … keep that in mind."

As he walked away, the dog turned to look at Hope, then back to Joe. Torn loyalties.

She watched Joe leave. The dog then placed her paw on Hope's foot, claiming ownership. Something soft unfurled inside her. She exhaled slowly.

It wasn't fear, and it wasn't dread.

Not trust, exactly, but the absence of threat.

And that was something.

CHAPTER 4

That evening, the café glowed in the way that Hope loved best, with low amber lights strung along the rafters and the scent of dough crisping in the oven.

She paused. This was the kind of warmth she used to dream about at night, when she huddled on the couch under quilts, too wary to sleep in her own bed. Now she was building something different. A place where people could feel safe and whole.

Hope glanced toward the back sink, where Ruby stood, sleeves rolled up and steam rising from the industrial tap. The girl moved stiffly, scrubbing a tray as if it had personally offended her.

"It's not a crime scene," Hope said gently, passing by with an order.

Ruby didn't look up. "It was really greasy."

"That's kind of the point. Good pizza leaves evidence."

The corner of Ruby's mouth twitched. Almost a smile.

The dinner crowd had started to arrive. Nothing wild, just a half-dozen young guys in flannel shirts and a group of older local women. Hope greeted them with her usual calm, but she could feel their glances towards the kitchen. A few eyes lingered on Ruby.

From the front table, old Mrs. Wilkinson leaned toward her friend and muttered just loudly enough: "That's Maureen's girl, isn't it? The one from the van parked on the field down behind the pub?"

Hope caught it, and so did Ruby. Her shoulders tightened, and her scrubbing became faster. Hope stepped behind the counter and poured a soda water with lime and a sprig of mint. She went and placed it beside Ruby at the sink, not just to refresh her, but to show anyone watching that Ruby belonged here.

"You're doing fine," she said. "They'll talk. That's what people do here. It doesn't mean they get to decide who you are."

Ruby didn't respond, but her scrubbing slowed.

***

Later, as Hope pulled pizzas out of the oven, she watched from the corner of her eye. Ruby moved like someone used to walking on eggshells: flinching slightly when the oven door slammed, shrinking away when a man laughed too loudly at a nearby table. Hope recognised all of it. The invisible language of someone trying to disappear.

After the rush, when the café had quieted and Hope was wiping down a table, Ruby hovered near the back door.

"Do I ... keep going?" she asked. "Or am I done?"

Hope looked up and nodded slowly. "You're free to go if you want. But there's leftover pumpkin and feta pizza if you're hungry."

Ruby hesitated. Her stomach growled loud enough to make her blush.

Hope put some pizza slices from the oven on a plate and placed it on the front counter. "You can eat in the kitchen if you'd rather not deal with the stares."

Ruby took it wordlessly, retreating to the back. Hope heard the soft creak of the stool and the clink of a plate. A long pause. Then words drifted out of the kitchen. "This is good. I don't remember the last time I tasted something like this."

Hope smiled to herself and kept wiping down tables.

She knew the signs of someone starving for more than just food.

"Where are you sleeping tonight?"

Hope let her question hang in the air as she went out to say goodbye to the last table of customers. When she returned to the kitchen, Ruby was just washing up her plate. Hope pushed open the door of the large storeroom next to the kitchen which had a mattress on the floor made up with sheets, a pillow and blanket.

"I used to bed down in here some nights when I was repainting the cottage and couldn't stand the paint fumes." Hope smiled at Ruby as she said, "It's nothing fancy, but it's warm. And safe."

"Aren't you worried that I'll take something and bolt?"

Hope paused, choosing her words. "I guess that's possible. But you'd be walking away from steady work and free hot meals here if you stay. So, it's up to you."

Ruby shrugged, still clinging to her defences. Then cautiously said, "I could just camp here tonight and see how I feel in the morning."

Hope nodded. "That sounds like a safe option."

After locking up the front door, Hope said goodnight to Ruby.

"Could I keep Asha with me?" Ruby asked, gesturing into the room.

Hope followed Ruby's hand to the stray, already curled up asleep in the corner of the storeroom.

"Asha?" Hope questioned.

"She's got ashy grey colours, like fireplace soot," Ruby explained.

Hope smiled. "It looks like she has already claimed her spot in here with you."

Ruby's eyes softened as she looked at the dog. "She makes me feel protected."

Hope nodded, her throat tightening as she locked the back door. "I'll see you both in the morning."

As Hope walked slowly across the backyard of the café to her cottage, she realised it felt different having Ruby and Asha sleeping on the property.

Maybe the trial wasn't just for Ruby, or the dog.

Perhaps, she was testing herself too.

To see if she was ready to start letting people back in.

CHAPTER 5

The café courtyard buzzed with noise and laughter, full of hungry customers of all shapes and sizes. Chairs scraped softly on the brick pavers, children darted amongst tables, and a chorus of happy barking echoed across the yard. The pizza oven crackled as Hope slid out another woodfired crust, the scent of basil and bubbling cheese drifting on the breeze.

Earlier that week, Ruby had gone to Joe's clinic with Asha to buy her a collar and lead. She'd overheard him mentioning the final Puppy Preschool class, and that's when the idea sparked. She'd suggested to Hope and Joe that the group come to *The Hearth* for a graduation celebration on Sunday afternoon.

Hope had been hesitant at first about having so many young dogs in the café backyard, but Ruby had been so enthusiastic, and surprisingly persuasive, that she'd agreed. "It'll be great for business," Ruby had said. So far, she'd been right.

"Next up—Coco!" Joe called with a grin, holding up a lopsided paper certificate.

A small dachshund in a dog burger costume bounded toward him, dragging her six-year-old owner, with a series of enthusiastic snorts. Laughter rippled through the group.

Ruby appeared with a fresh jug of sparkling lemon myrtle water, refilling glasses and offering napkins as she moved around.

"Second costume change for Coco," Ruby whispered to Hope with a smirk, brushing flour from her arm.

"She's setting the bar high," Hope murmured, watching the girl lift her pup in front of the small crowd.

Ruby had thrown herself into planning. She'd baked puppy biscuits, sketched a themed pizza menu, and even drafted a rough afternoon program. It was amazing to see her blossom so quickly in a space where she felt safe and useful.

Now, as Hope watched her weaving through the group gathered on picnic blankets and courtyard chairs, she noticed how easily Ruby remembered every name, both human and canine. It seemed to come naturally. Hope made a mental note of it. Ruby had a gift: for names, for people, for finding her place in the moments that mattered.

By the time the last "graduate" had been patted and praised, the courtyard was full of conversation and the warm glow of shared joy.

Someone called out, "You should do this every week!"

Hope half-laughed, wiping her hands on a tea towel.

Ruby, eyes sparkling as she collected empty glasses, leaned towards Hope with a grin. "What if we did? Pets & Pizza Sundays—crusts for humans, crumbs for canines."

Laughter rippled again, followed by nearby murmurs of agreement.

"I'd come," said a young mum, scratching behind her beagle pup's ears. "So would Rocket."

Others chimed in, saying they had friends with well-behaved dogs who'd love to come to a regular Sunday pizza afternoon in the café yard.

Joe caught Hope's eye and raised his brows. "Could be something," he said, his tone low and easy.

Hope shrugged, aiming for casual. But something fluttered, unfamiliar and light, like hope testing its wings. The joy in the courtyard felt real. Earned. And maybe ... repeatable.

***

Later, after the last of the pet owners left the yard, Ruby wiped down tables and emptied water bowls. She worked with a quiet happiness, like small things carried real weight.

Ruby glanced up and said enthusiastically, "We could have a 'Dog of the Week' photo wall, have leftover crusts in a jar for dogs, or even a custom chalkboard menu for dog-safe snacks?"

Hope gave a slow nod, remembering how Ruby's eyes had lit up earlier and how easily she connected with the locals. As she stood there watching Ruby, for the first time Hope started to think of her not as a stray teen, but as part of the team she wanted to build here at the café.

She took a step closer and said gently, "Ruby, how old are you?"

Ruby didn't flinch at the question. While scrubbing at a splash of pesto on the table, she said, "I turned eighteen last month."

Hope nodded slowly. "And your mum? She's still in town?"

Ruby's shoulders stiffened just slightly. "Yeah. She's in that old caravan behind the pub. It's not really safe there. Her boyfriend's got a temper, and ... I just couldn't stay."

Hope didn't press. She just let the words land and settle between them, heavy but not unbearable.

"Well," she said, "why don't you go inside when you're finished and jot down your pet customer ideas?" She paused, then added with a small smile, "I think you might be part of our new marketing team."

Ruby beamed at the praise and nearly skipped as she headed inside.

As the sun was just stretching its last rays across the valley, Joe stayed to put chairs back around the tables. There was a companionable silence between himself and Hope.

After a few minutes, Hope spoke softly ... almost to herself. "I didn't expect to enjoy this afternoon with all that noise and chaos."

Joe waited a few beats, then replied gently, meeting her gaze, "Joy can be loud too."

Hope looked away and nodded.

Joe didn't want to press. Instead, he lightened the moment by gesturing toward Ruby, who could be seen sitting inside through the café's back door, hunched over a notepad with a pencil between her fingers and a grin on her face.

"I think you might have found yourself quite a gem there."

Hope looked in at her. She noticed the way Ruby's brow furrowed as she sketched out ideas, the way her whole body leaned toward the possibility of something good. "You're not wrong," she said quietly.

There was a pause. Hope glanced down at the cloth in her hands, then added, her voice softer now, "She can't live at home, it's ... not safe. She's had to grow up fast."

Joe's smile faded into something steadier. He just nodded.

"Thanks for your encouragement in making this afternoon happen," Hope said.

"It's all part of the service in being a local small-town vet," Joe replied lightly as he turned to go. He stopped at the edge of the gate and looked back, smiling. "You're building more than a café, Hope."

Before she could reply, he turned again and called out, "See you, Ruby!" through the open door. Ruby waved without looking up.

Hope watched him walk away, his figure steady in the fading light, and then turned back to the warm glow inside. To look at the girl with a messy ponytail and a page full of ideas who had already started to feel like family.

***

Later that night, the café sat quietly again, shadows from the lights over the counter stretching long across the timber floors. Hope ran the cloth around areas still dusted with flour and flecked with pieces of basil. Walking past the storeroom, she paused to look in and saw Ruby and Asha curled up together on the mattress.

She reached for her notepad, scribbled down the words *Pets & Pizza Sundays?* and pinned it to the fridge with the old paw-print magnet Ruby had found in a drawer and left strategically on the bench for her to see.

Hope stood back, brushing hands on her apron. She wasn't sure if this was her saying yes to letting people in, but it felt close. And for now, close was enough.

She clicked off the lights, one by one, until only the fairy lights outside in the backyard glowed above the café tables, soft, golden and waiting.

CHAPTER 6

The café was quiet on Monday mornings. It was Hope's chosen day to rest from customers, to catch up on orders and bake cakes for the week ahead. A slow exhale after the weekend. The rush of Sunday had passed, leaving the scents of baking in the air.

Hope had just finished a flourless orange and almond cake that was cooling on the kitchen bench. She came out to see Asha who was sprawled beneath the front counter, her soft snoring a rhythm that Ruby seemed to match. Ruby was curled in a sunny corner of the café on the floor, with a sketchbook open and a teacup going cold.

Hope began restocking the tea shelf when the bell above the door jingled softly. Glancing at the clock, Hope wiped her hands on a towel and turned around.

A fit and slender kind-eyed man in his early fifties walked towards the counter, smiling.

"Hope Elkins?" he asked in a warm, rumbling voice. "Sorry to drop in unannounced. I'm Tom. Pastor Tom Harvey. From the community church in town."

Hope stiffened slightly. "Oh. Yes, hi. I've … seen you around."

Pastor Tom looked around the café, nodding approvingly.

"I realise you are closed today, but I hope you don't mind me quickly popping in."

Hope straightened, already bracing herself. She forced a politeness. "Not at all."

Tom spoke sincerely. "The place looks great. You've done so much work. I think your grandmother would have been so proud of you."

Hope felt emotions rising at the mention of her grandmother and swallowed them back down. She wasn't sure if this was a compliment or the lead-in to something heavier.

Tom continued, "Edith's mentioned you to me a few times. Told me you're finding your way back home, and that you're making this café into something more than a business."

Hope raised an eyebrow. "She's always been a cheerleader for me. Even from afar."

Tom grinned. "She's got the spiritual gift of connection, whether it's souls, stories, or new friendships."

Hope rolled her eyes. "Please tell me she didn't mention Joe Butler to you."

"She only mentioned that he's been turning up at your café like a stray."

Despite herself, Hope laughed.

Tom's tone softened. "The truth is, I came to let you know that if at any stage you feel ready, we'd love to welcome you to visit our church community. We have a women's group that meets on Thursday evenings. It's low-key. Tea and coffee, a bit of Bible reading together. It's not perfect, but it's real. You'd be welcome."

Hope looked down at the counter, her heart thudding a little too hard.

She wasn't ready for Bible study, group prayer, open wounds, or well-meaning platitudes.

"I'm not sure," she said honestly. "Church feels … complicated."

Tom nodded, pausing before he quietly spoke. "God's not complicated. People are. And He's very patient with them."

Hope bit her lip. "I appreciate the invitation. I'm just not sure where I stand with all of it yet."

"That's okay." He reached into his coat and pulled out a brown paper bag. "My wife Eve thought you might find this helpful." He pulled a slim book out of the bag: *Grace in the Broken Places.*

Hope's smile didn't fade, but it wavered, hesitant. She ran her thumb along the edge of the cover. "That's thoughtful."

Pastor Tom spoke kindly. "We've also got a small group that meets at the church monthly, women who've walked through some hard places. They are meeting next Monday evening at 6pm. No pressure. Just a cuppa and real conversation."

Hope didn't answer immediately. She heard Ruby stand and drift closer, curiosity flickering in her eyes. Asha stirred, her tail began thumping softly against the timber floor.

"Thanks," she said at last. "I'll think about it."

Tom stepped back toward the door. "And Hope?"

She looked up.

"When you're ready, you don't have to find your way back to God. He's already on the road with you."

The bell jingled again as he left.

***

The sun was warm on the gravel path, and the café's front garden stirred with the scent of thyme and lavender. Asha bounded across the open space, tail high, ears flopping, chasing the stick Ruby had flung with more energy than she usually had in the mornings.

Hope knelt a little further back among her herb beds, gently loosening the soil around a pot of parsley, the soft rustle of leaves and the low hum of bees keeping her company. She couldn't hear what Ruby was chatting to Asha about but smiled at the girl's warm affection for the dog that was growing daily.

Ruby brushed wind-blown hair from her face, watching Asha run back with the stick. "Good girl," she murmured, crouching to ruffle the dog's scruffy ears.

A familiar voice called from the street.

"Looks like she's got you well trained," Joe said, leaning on the timber post out the front, his smile easy and warm.

Ruby straightened, her smile pulling at her mouth. "She's got lots of energy."

Joe stepped closer, crouching to pat Asha, then glancing up at Ruby. "How are you settling in?"

Ruby hesitated, shoulders giving a small shrug. "I'm thinking I might stay around here for a while." She glanced sideways at Asha. "I sleep better when she's near."

Joe nodded thoughtfully. "Animals do that. They help us regulate and model healthy life patterns like needing play and rest. And they instinctively know who is safe to trust."

He reached into his coat pocket and handed Asha a small treat, which she gobbled up enthusiastically.

"We've got a quiet little program at the church," he added. "Pet companionship. Nothing fancy. We visit elderly folks who are shut in and lonely. Some haven't had a proper conversation all week, until a dog walks through the door. It softens something."

Ruby tilted her head, curious. "You mean … people just want to see a dog?"

Joe chuckled. "More than you'd think. Dogs bring warmth without words. Just showing up can change things. My chocolate Labrador, Bounty, knows how to charm all the elderly ladies."

Ruby was quiet for a moment. Asha nosed at her palm, and she absently stroked the Aussie Shepherd's head.

"Could I do that?" she asked quietly. "Visit someone, I mean. With Asha."

Joe studied her face, careful not to crowd the moment. "I think you'd be really good at it."

A breeze passed through the garden, stirring the scents of basil and gum leaves.

"I just …" Ruby looked down, then back up. "I want to give something back. Even if it's small. Asha and I, we've helped each other. Maybe we could help someone else feel … not so alone."

Behind the herb patch, Hope's hands had stilled. She'd heard their conversation and looked up through the rosemary, watching Ruby as if seeing her for the first time. She began to see her not just as a fragile guest under her roof, or a girl in need, but as someone with a soul full of quiet wisdom. Someone hurt, yes, but also someone reaching out to give.

Hope felt her throat tighten. There was a kind of healing that didn't always start with therapy or books or even prayer. Sometimes it started with a dog, and a stick, and the simple desire to make someone else feel seen.

***

Later that evening, Hope looked out from her cottage. The café had been empty all day, but the stillness now felt different. Heavier, quieter. The stars were scattered sharp and clear above the gum trees, and a breeze moved gently through the jacaranda, rustling the leaves like whispers.

Barefoot at the door, Hope stood wrapped in an old cardigan, a mug of tea cooling in her hands. The faint glow from the café windows across the yard was comforting. She could just make out a sliver of light beneath the storeroom door in Ruby's makeshift room and imagined the familiar shape of Asha's silhouette sitting inside.

Hope was glad Ruby had the dog. And the space. Even if it was temporary. Even if none of them were quite sure what came next.

Her gaze dropped to the small table near her cottage door. *Grace in the Broken Places* sat where she'd left it, the brown paper bag now folded neatly beneath it. She hadn't touched it all day, but somehow it still felt like it was waiting.

She picked it up slowly, weighing it in her hands as if she was measuring its worth. The cover was soft to the touch. It had cool blues, with the picture of a shaft of light through a broken windowpane.

She sank into the armchair by her hearth, the coals still faintly warm from earlier. Silence wrapped around her, not unfriendly, just … watchful. She hadn't expected to be moved by Ruby's quiet courage today. Or by Joe's soft steadiness. But something had stirred. Enough to open the book.

She half-expected it to feel too neat, or preachy. But the first page made her pause.

"To those still standing in the rubble, unsure if grace can reach them there."

Her fingers closed over the edges of the page. She looked toward the window again, to the soft glow of the café and the quiet life growing inside it.

She didn't feel ready for faith. Not in the traditional sense. But she did feel … hollowed out. Like a field after fire. And maybe that was a place to begin again from.

She opened the book again, looked at just one page, one quiet beginning, and let the words find her in the stillness.

***

The following afternoon, the sun was dipping low behind the trees, casting long shadows across the gravel drive outside a weatherboard cottage. Joe leaned against the ute parked by the fence while Hope stood beside him, arms loosely crossed, watching.

Ruby had asked Hope to come along, but at the last minute asked if she could try visiting Anne Lucas alone. Ruby was now standing on her porch; Asha close by her side. She held a small paper bag—Hope had seen her pack it with leftover muffins that morning, insisting they were too good to waste.

Anne opened the door with a cautious smile, one hand braced on the screen. "You with the church?"

Ruby nodded. "Sort of." She gestured towards the car. "Joe runs the program. I'm just … showing up."

She hadn't over-explained or tried to be charming. Just stood there, awkward and real, until Asha stepped forward and placed her front paws gently on the door mat, tail wagging low and slow.

Anne's face softened. "Well, now. Aren't you a beautiful girl?"

Within minutes, the three of them were seated on the verandah. Ruby was perched on the step, Asha nestled at Anne's feet. Ruby handed over the muffins with shy pride. Anne poured tea from an old teapot and began to talk. About her garden. Her late husband. And her chickens recently being attacked by foxes.

Ruby listened.

Hope watched from the roadside. She could see that Ruby's posture, with shoulders relaxed and eyes soft, showed that she wasn't performing. She was simply there.

Joe glanced at Hope. "She's better with people than she realises."

Hope nodded, swallowing against a sudden lump in her throat. She remembered it had been only a few weeks ago that Ruby was a girl who could barely look her in the eye.

"She's giving herself to people," Hope said, more to herself than to Joe.

They stood there in silence for a few moments, watching the unlikely trio share tea, crumbs, and quiet company in the fading light.

Hope thought of the book again, and the quiet words from last night she hadn't yet let in.

You don't have to be whole to be welcomed. Just willing.

Maybe Ruby wasn't the only one showing up.

Hope wondered if she was almost ready, too.

CHAPTER 7

Hope stepped into the courtyard, balancing a tray of orders. Their first official Pets & Pizza Sunday had drawn families, older couples, and a scattering of four-legged guests. She smiled at the low-level chaos, weaving between tables as she served.

Her eyes were watchful, reading interactions and gauging tensions. She stayed alert, ready to step in if needed.

At the far end, under the mulberry tree, sat Joe Butler. This time he had two animals with him. A faithful chocolate Labrador, who was drumming his tail on the grass, watching a tiny ginger kitten in a travel crate.

"You're starting a zoo?" Hope asked as she placed a plate in front of him.

"Working on it," Joe said, smiling up at her. He pointed to the kitten. "This little girl was found in a storm drain by the bakery. Someone's gotta foster her. Bounty here would love us to have her, but my little cottage is already crowded with the two of us."

Hope glanced at the kitten, barely the size of a croissant. "She doesn't seem to take up much space. Are you sure you can't squeeze her in?"

"Well …" He shrugged. "Only until someone else steps up. It's another week of bottle-feeding every few hours. Then she can start eating kitten food."

Hope raised an eyebrow.

"I see where this is going."

"Just think about it," he said, grin widening.

"As it's my day off tomorrow, I can take her to cover the feeds tonight," she said. "But I'm not committing to a third dependent unless she promises not to wake the whole house."

Joe's grin deepened. "You're already a soft touch. You'll name her before the end of the night."

Hope opened her mouth to reply but paused as a sharp bark rang out, followed by the soft clatter of a tipped water bowl. A small dachshund in a sequinned vest bounded towards a crust on the ground, knocking the water bowl sideways across the pavers.

A child giggled nearby. A budgie in its cage on a table gave a startled chirp. The air held the scent of fresh basil and damp fur.

Hope turned to help, but someone was already turning over the water bowl. She was a young woman in her late twenties, wearing a fitted cardigan and a dark ponytail of curls. There was a tiredness behind her eyes that made Hope suddenly more watchful.

"Sorry about that," the woman said quickly, reaching for extra napkins. "Daisy gets overexcited."

The dachshund looked entirely unrepentant, snuffling someone's dropped pizza crust.

"No harm done," Hope said warmly. "With the first Pets and Pizza Sunday, chaos was always part of the plan."

The woman smiled, though it didn't reach her eyes. A little girl, who was maybe six, clung to her skirt, peeking out from behind her legs. She wore gumboots and a tutu, and her face was painted like a butterfly.

"She's Daisy's stylist," the woman added, ruffling her daughter's curls. "I'm Nova. This is Lily."

Hope crouched a little to meet the girl's gaze. "Nice to meet you both. I love your butterfly wings, Lily."

The child gave a shy nod. Nova stroked her daughter's hair absently, glancing toward the gate.

Hope followed her gaze. A man stood by the front fence. He was tall, clean-cut, arms crossed. Watching. Something about his stance, too still and too confident, prickled Hope's skin. Under her gaze, he turned and walked back towards the road.

Nova straightened quickly. "We should probably get going."

Hope's instincts flared. She touched Nova's arm lightly. "Stay. You've barely had a slice. And we've just pulled out the mulberry and pear crumble. It's on the house for all the first timers."

Nova hesitated.

"I've got a quiet table by the hedge," Hope offered. "Lots of space for Daisy to sniff around."

After a moment, Nova nodded. "Thanks."

***

Later, the sun had dropped behind the hills. Fairy lights strung through the trees began to glow. Ruby brought out marshmallows for the kids to toast at the fire pit. Joe now had a second kitten on his lap. The Labrador was asleep against his foot.

Hope moved between tables, topping up drinks and checking plates, but her eye kept drifting to Nova.

She sat stiffly, eating slowly, with Lily curled up beside her.

At one point, when Nova rose to help her daughter wash her hands, Hope followed her inside.

"I can tell you're being careful," Hope said gently. "If you ever need someone to talk to … or somewhere safe, my door's open."

Nova blinked fast. "I'm fine."

Hope didn't push. "All right. Just so you know, you're not alone."

Nova gave a tiny nod and returned to the courtyard, telling Lily it was time for them to go.

***

When the last guests had gone and Ruby was in the café kitchen with Asha, Hope sat beside Joe beneath the mulberry tree. The ginger kitten was now curled in her lap, purring like a tractor.

"Nova was scared," Hope said quietly. "But she stayed."

Joe looked toward the gate. "Sometimes that's the bravest thing."

The silence between them was soft and familiar. The fire pit burned low, glowing beneath charred logs.

Hope hesitated. The words caught in her throat like something too dry to swallow. But the firelight, the quiet and the way Joe didn't push, made her speak as she stared into the flames. "I remember that look, the way Nova kept glancing over her shoulder. I used to do that. I lived in fear … but also in denial."

Joe didn't interrupt. He just waited.

"I spent years trying to stay safe from his moods, and his words. Trying to be *enough*. Kind. Patient. Anything that might keep the peace. The house was full of tension. And still, I stayed."

She traced a finger gently along the kitten's spine.

"But in the end, he didn't choose to finish it. He just started seeing someone else. Kept coming home late, gaslighting me. I only found out when I saw the messages on his iPad."

Joe's jaw tightened, but he stayed quiet.

"Funny, isn't it?" she said. "I probably wouldn't have left unless he'd cheated. That was the final line I couldn't explain away." She stared into the fire. "But the line had been crossed years earlier. I just … couldn't see it."

The embers crackled softly.

"He was turning the heat up so slowly you didn't notice," Joe said gently.

Hope nodded. "That's what makes the healing so slow. You stop trusting your own judgement. And you grieve who you could have been."

Joe's voice was quiet. "And what you hoped the marriage would become."

She turned toward Joe, taking him in fully. No judgement. No pressure. Just the kind of steadiness she hadn't dared to trust in a long time.

"I don't know if I believe in second chances yet," she said.

"There's no rush," Joe replied.

They sat there side by side in the hush of the evening.

Hope wondered … maybe her story wasn't over. Maybe she was just turning a page.

CHAPTER 8

The sky was still the colour of cold ash when Hope reversed her SUV out of the café's driveway, headlights cutting through the early fog that clung to the paddocks. The air outside was brisk for an autumn morning, so the insulated mug of chai Hope handed Ruby had steam curling up like smoke.

"Remind me again why markets start at dawn?" Ruby muttered, as she tried to warm up her hands.

Hope smirked. "Because tomatoes don't sleep in."

The car rattled slightly as they hit a stretch of road under repair, shifting the empty boxes and bags in the back. Ruby yawned behind her hand. Her legs were tucked under her on the passenger seat.

A few kilometres out, the road dipped into a hollow flanked by bushland. Hope reached to change the radio but instead braked suddenly.

"What?"

"Echidna," Hope said, pointing.

On the narrow road ahead, the creature trundled across with complete disregard for traffic, spines bristling like a living hairbrush. Hope flicked on the hazards and pulled halfway off the road to let it pass.

They watched in silence as it disappeared into the long grass.

"You've never seen one before, have you?" Ruby asked.

"Only in wildlife parks. They're usually hard to spot."

"That one was on a mission."

Hope grinned. "Same as us. Tomatoes or bust."

The moment lingered behind them like the mist as they drove on.

By the time they reached the growers market, the sky had softened to blue, and the field was filling with people in gumboots and linen aprons. Hope manoeuvred the SUV into a spot near the stables and opened the boot.

"Okay," she said, checking the list she'd scribbled on the back of an envelope. "Root veg, heirloom tomatoes, maybe some preserves. And if you see anything that might be inspiring for cake recipes, call it out."

"Copy that," Ruby said, stretching.

The market buzzed with colour and chatter. The stalls were stacked with dirt-dusted vegetables, bunches of greens, and chalk signs offering fresh farm eggs and marinated olives.

Ruby perked up as she spotted a coffee and doughnut van. Her mood seemed to lift. She then held up a giant Japanese pumpkin for Hope to admire.

"I think this place is growing on me," Ruby said.

Hope smiled. "Meeting the hands that grow the food, it does something. Grounds you."

But that ease vanished the moment they reached the goat farmer's stall.

The smell hit hard: pungent raw meat and smoke, with goat kofta kebabs sizzling on a grill. Ruby stopped mid-step, face suddenly pale.

"You okay?" Hope asked.

"Yeah. Fine," Ruby said, though one hand clutched at her stomach.

She turned away, eyes unfocused, toward a display of apples like she might be sick. Hope gave her space but stayed close.

"You sure?"

Ruby nodded too fast. "Some days I wonder if I should just go vegetarian."

Hope didn't press.

They were elbow-deep in tomatoes, plump yellow ones, like sunshine, and deep red Oxhearts that were broad and knobbly, when a voice rang out behind them.

"Well, if it isn't Ruby Anne. Out of bed before noon. That's a rare sight."

Hope turned.

A woman in a stiff denim jacket stood holding a punnet of strawberries, hair streaked with purple dye and eyes sharpened by years of bitterness. Her smile didn't reach them.

Ruby froze.

"Mum."

Hope blinked. *This* was Maureen.

There wasn't much resemblance. At least, nothing warm. Maybe the jawline. But the woman's whole stance was defensive and pointed.

"I heard you were still lurking in Wombat Valley," Maureen said, eyeing the stall. "What's this? Got yourself a job now?"

Hope stepped in, casually but firm. "I'm Hope. I run *The Hearth Café*. Ruby helps me out there."

Maureen gave her a long look. Her smile thinned. "Do you staff it with charity cases?"

Ruby stiffened.

Hope's voice didn't rise. "Ruby's not a case. She's smart, capable, and a key part of what we do."

Maureen gave a clipped laugh. "Well, she must be eating well on your payroll. You've *filled out*, Rubes."

Hope looked at Ruby. She saw the gentle curves that had grown on her lean body since she'd started eating regularly. She smiled warmly. "She's healthy. And she looks strong. The kind of strong people notice, for the right reasons."

Maureen rolled her eyes. "Please. She's never had trouble getting attention. That was half the problem, wasn't it?"

She turned back to Ruby. "Still seeing that counsellor I told you was a waste of money?"

Ruby's voice was low. "No, Mum."

"Good. Told you it was useless. You always did love the drama."

Hope's hands clenched in her coat pockets. She didn't move, didn't speak. Just stood beside Ruby like a shield.

Ruby said nothing. Just stared down at the tomatoes, knuckles white.

Maureen shifted her feet. "Well, I'd best get going. Paul doesn't like it when I'm out too long."

Ruby flinched at the name.

"Still in the caravan?" she asked, softly.

Maureen sniffed. "Better than some of the places we've been."

She turned away before leaving, pausing just long enough to say, "You should call sometime. Don't be a stranger."

And with that, she disappeared down the row of stalls, clicking her tongue at the price of potatoes.

They stood in silence.

Hope didn't push. She handed Ruby a slice of ripe fig from a stall where the owner had pink wind-chapped cheeks and kind eyes.

When they got back to the SUV, Ruby climbed into the passenger seat and shut the door a little too hard.

Hope started the engine but didn't drive.

"She shouldn't talk to you like that."

Ruby stared straight ahead. "She doesn't know how *not* to."

Hope hesitated, then reached into her handbag and pulled out a small packet of locally dried pears. It was something she'd seen Ruby eyeing earlier.

"For you."

Ruby took it slowly, her fingers brushing Hope's. "Thanks."

They drove in silence for a while.

Then Hope said, "She doesn't get to decide who you become."

Ruby didn't look at her. But after a few seconds, she whispered, "Thank you."

When they arrived back at the café, the boot full of food and the silence between them somehow felt heavy … and light. Like clear sky after a storm. Like a decision had just been made.

Hope started unloading crates.

Before she could reach for the tomatoes, Ruby turned and hugged her. It was quick, almost clumsy, but fierce.

Hope's arms froze in surprise. She hadn't seen it coming, but she didn't pull away.

"I've got you," she said quietly. "Whatever comes next."

Ruby didn't speak.

But held on for a moment longer.

***

Journal Entry – Saturday Evening

Maureen.

I saw the shape of Ruby's history today. She was brittle, sharp-edged, and hollow in all the wrong places. Her mother discarded Ruby's pain like it was nothing. Like a crumpled receipt, tossed aside and forgotten.

And still, Ruby stood there. She didn't argue. Just absorbed the bitterness. Like she's probably done for most of her life.

And I felt a quiet, heavy resolve. To be different. To offer more. To be a place, not just another person who passes through.

I used to think not becoming a mother in the traditional way meant I'd missed that chance. But maybe that kind of love has more than one door.

Can it begin by simply making space for someone else?

Does it look like offering shelter, or chai on cold mornings, or standing between someone and a history that still echoes too loud?

I can't erase the past. But I can help shape the future.

Maybe that's the kind of mother I get to be.

Maybe that's enough.

H.

CHAPTER 9

*H*ope stepped into the empty vet clinic, sunlight striping the floor through the front windows.

A "Back in 5 mins," sign sat on the counter, though she could hear the faint sounds of movement from somewhere down the hall.

Hope hesitated, pizza box warm in her hands, unsure if she was intruding or if a chat would be welcome.

"Joe?" she called.

A soft thud came from down the hall. Tired, not urgent footsteps.

Joe appeared in the doorway, wearing scrubs, his eyes shadowed with fatigue. He blinked when he saw her. "Hope. What …?"

"I come bearing gifts," she said tentatively, lifting the box. "Woodfired. Extra olives. And the fancy ginger beer."

His expression flickered somewhere between surprise and exhaustion. "You didn't have to."

"I know," she said simply. "But I haven't seen you this week. There's been no new strays dropped on our doorstep." She then spoke honestly. "You've been keeping an eye out for us … so I'm returning the favour."

He stepped aside and gestured toward the staff kitchen. "Come through."

The room smelled faintly of eucalyptus disinfectant and dog biscuits. A kettle sat idle on the counter. On the floor in the corner lay a small cardboard box with a pet crematorium label.

Joe caught her glance, then exhaled with a long sigh.

"She was only seven months old," he said, opening the pizza and tearing off a slice, though he didn't eat. "Came in from a rescue centre. Sweet little thing. I thought she was pulling through."

Hope didn't speak, just took a seat across from him at the dining table and waited.

"She was meant to go back tomorrow," he added, eyes fixed on a knot in the timber. "Sometimes it feels like you do everything right ... and they still die."

He rubbed at his temple, jaw tightening.

"It's not just this week. It sneaks up on me sometimes. The losses. Even the ones I thought I'd already dealt with."

She set the paper bag between them and pulled out two glass bottles.

"Drink something. You look exhausted, you probably need sugar."

He cracked one open and took a long sip, then spoke, softly.

"I lost my wife Anna ... two winters ago."

Hope looked up.

"She had ovarian cancer. It was ... fast. Six months between diagnosis and ..." He trailed off, then exhaled slowly.

"She never stopped planning things for after. Lists. Bookmarked trips. Told me I'd laugh again someday."

He gave a faint smile. "I thought she was being naive. Or noble. But now I think ... she just knew I'd need a reason to keep going."

Hope reached for her own bottle in the centre of the table, her fingers brushing his as she did. He didn't pull away.

"I'm sorry, Joe."

He nodded. Not out of politeness, but in understanding.

"It still hurts me. When animals die. Even now. Some just ... land really hard. And I don't always know what to do with it."

Hope studied him for a moment. She saw his broad shoulders, a hint of silver edging into his hairline, the way he carried stillness like a coat, and the creases around his careful quiet eyes.

"You always seem so steady," she said.

"I'm not. I just learned how to carry it and keep going."

Her voice dropped.

"I used to think I was the only one walking around with ghosts."

Joe looked at her then, fully.

"Do you want to share them with me?"

She hesitated. "I lost my dad when I was ten. Mum died four years ago. Cancer, like Anna."

Joe's eyes softened.

"That's a lot to carry."

He paused, then added: "I turned forty just after she died. It felt like standing on the edge of something I never planned for."

Hope gave a small nod.

"I was thirty-one when Mum passed. She never got to see me leave Mark. She was worried about my safety, but I kept waiting for things to get better. Until I realised they wouldn't."

They sat in silence. The sun dipped lower through the blinds, streaking the wall in amber light.

On the shelf behind him, Hope noticed a small photograph. It was Joe and a woman with dark hair and laughing eyes, windblown, standing on a rocky outcrop with the Labrador at their feet. It was unframed, tucked in the corner like something you didn't need to see to remember.

"She would've liked you," Joe said, catching her glance.

Something swelled in Hope's chest. A feeling that was unexpected, tender, and steadying.

"Thank you. That means more than you know."

After a few more quiet minutes, Joe pushed the pizza box toward her. "Take it back for Ruby. She'll eat the anchovies if you don't."

She stood, gathering the box and bottles, but paused at the door. "Thanks for letting me in."

Joe gave a small nod.

"Thanks for coming. And for not pretending it's all okay."

Hope hesitated.

"We're all a little not fine. But we don't have to be alone."

Joe smiled and nodded.

As she stepped outside into the light of late afternoon, the air smelled of gum trees and dust. The world hadn't changed, but something in her had. Hope felt she wasn't just carrying her own grief anymore. Maybe sharing their stories had built a bridge. One strong enough to carry them both.

***

When Hope returned, the café was in between hours. Shadows were long across the timber floor. The prep bench still bore traces of flour, and the faint scent of rosemary and tomato hung in the air.

She set down the pizza box on the counter and slid off her cardigan. Ruby looked up from the coffee machine she was wiping down.

"Back finally," she said. "I was about to start drafting a missing person's report."

Hope smiled, caught off guard. "I wasn't gone that long."

"You left with a mysterious bag and a box that smelled like anchovies." Ruby raised an eyebrow. "That's suspicious behaviour."

Hope pulled two empty ginger beer bottles from the bag. "I went to check on Joe."

Ruby paused. "Oh."

"I hadn't seen him for a few days. Just thought I'd … bring him something. He's had a rough week."

Ruby nodded slowly, leaning her hip against the counter. "So, was it a check-on-him visit or a check-on-your-heart visit?"

Hope blinked. "Excuse me?"

Ruby smirked, but the teasing was gentle. "You're different when you've been talking to him."

Hope opened her mouth to reply. Then she closed it again.

"I'm not saying you're swooning or whatever," Ruby added quickly. "Just … you're quieter. Calmer. You look less like you're carrying the weight of the world."

Hope let out a breath. "Is it that obvious?"

"Only to someone who lives in your storeroom and has a black belt in reading emotions," Ruby said lightly, then turned more serious. "He's good, Hope. Joe. The quiet kind. Someone who shows up."

Hope leaned back against the bench. "Yeah. He is."

Ruby picked at the corner of a serviette, then glanced up. "He doesn't talk much. But when he does, it means something. Like last week when he helped me calm Asha down when she got tangled in the fruit tree netting. He didn't say much. He just crouched down and untied her, talking quietly, keeping her calm. He shares wisdom with me about animals that applies to people too."

Hope paused thoughtfully, then said, "he told me about his wife today."

Ruby's eyes softened. "Anna?"

"You knew?"

"He keeps a photo of her on his noticeboard. And there's this weird half-dead pot plant in the corner with a tag that says 'Anna's herb' in faded ink. I asked once and he just said, 'she liked things wild.'" Ruby smiled faintly. "He also jokes that Anna named their dog Bounty because it was

49

her favourite chocolate bar, but says the name fits because their Lab's a bit nuts on the inside. It's almost like … she's still there with him."

Hope swallowed. "It's strange. I keep thinking I'm the only one with pain shaped like a shadow."

"You're not," Ruby said, matter of fact.

That stopped Hope cold.

Ruby shrugged, brushing crumbs into her palm. "It's okay, you know. To still be sad or angry. Even when things are good. Even when life starts feeling safe again."

Hope looked at her, not just as the troubled teen she'd taken in, but as someone older on the inside than she should be.

"You're getting wise on me," she murmured.

"I blame the caffeine fumes. And that box of old devotional books you left in the café storeroom. Too hard to keep in the cottage, huh?" Ruby challenged playfully. "Also, watching you. You're softer now. Not in a weak way. Just … open."

Hope let those words settle. Then: "You really think so?"

Ruby nodded. "I used to think no one made it out of a troubled relationship without getting mean or numb. But you're proving maybe there's another option."

Hope reached out and touched her arm. "You might just be the best part of my second chapter."

Ruby grinned. "Well, I'll take the anchovies off your hands. That counts for something, right?"

Hope laughed, and without overthinking it, reached out to squeeze her shoulders in a hug.

CHAPTER 10

The morning rush had passed. The café was quieter now, with a few locals reading newspapers and dogs asleep beside tables out the front. Hope was restocking the display cabinet with a pear and almond tart when the bell over the door tinkled.

Hope looked up, her smile automatic. Then she focused on what Joe was holding.

It was a faded green notebook, its corners were frayed and the spine bound in old masking tape. A single stalk of rosemary was tucked within its pages.

Hope straightened slowly. "Morning."

Joe nodded. "Brought you something. Thought you might like it."

He stepped forward and set the book on the counter between them like it was something fragile. Reverent. Hope looked down. For a moment, the whole world stilled.

On the cover, in looping handwriting, "Anna's Cakes—My favourites." Underneath was a little hand-drawn sketch of a whisk and a heart.

"I thought ..." Joe began, then stopped, clearing his throat. "She'd have liked this place. I think she would've loved to see someone bringing her recipes back to life."

Hope ran her fingers gently over the cover, like she was touching someone's journal. "Joe, are you sure?"

He nodded, quiet but sure. "Just don't spill sauce on it. She'd haunt us both."

Hope smiled, though her throat felt tight. "I'll take care of it."

"She baked for school fundraisers, the church … and anyone breathing, really. Half the time she'd forget to write down the actual temperature, so you'll have to guess a bit."

"I can probably do the guesswork," Hope said softly.

Joe looked at her, not with intensity, but with that same quiet depth that had started to feel like a shelter. "I know."

***

The notebook sat on Hope's kitchen bench like a sleeping treasure. She hadn't yet opened it. She wasn't sure she was ready.

There was something deeply significant about the idea of it, the handwritten legacy of a woman who was gone but still deeply loved. And here it was, entrusted to her. Part of her wanted to dive in; part of her was afraid of where it might lead.

Then Ruby burst through the back door, Asha following at a trot, nosing the air.

"What's that?" Ruby asked, as she tossed her backpack onto the bench.

Hope placed a gentle hand over the notebook. "It was Anna's. Her cake recipes handwritten."

Ruby's eyes widened. "Like, her actual handwriting?"

Hope nodded. "Every page."

Ruby leaned over the bench. "Can we open it?"

Hope hesitated. Then opened the cover.

The pages were filled with ink and pencil, some smudged, with little notes in the margins. "Might need more lemon zest," "Good for cold winter mornings", "Never leave unattended, burnt once when distracted by Bounty in the yard."

Ruby laughed softly. "She sounds really down to earth."

Hope smiled. "She does."

Ruby flipped through until one recipe caught her eye. "Anna's Apricot Tea Loaf—makes two, always give one away."

"I want to try this one," Ruby said.

Hope raised an eyebrow. "You're going to bake?"

"I've watched you enough times. I've got this." Ruby stood and reached for the mixing bowls. "Besides, it says to give one away. That feels like something we'd do here."

Hope watched her, her heart full, and throat tight. Maybe this was how love was passed on. Through family recipes, and margin notes left behind.

***

The café smelled of apricots and brown sugar. Ruby stood at the kitchen bench, cheeks flushed, flour dusting her shirt like snow. Hope was wiping down the display cabinet when she noticed Ruby carefully wrapping the second loaf in brown paper and tying it with kitchen twine.

"Where's that one going?" Hope asked.

Ruby shrugged. "It said give one away. So, I'm giving it."

Hope set the cloth down. "To who?"

Ruby hesitated. "Nova."

Hope blinked. "*Nova?*"

"She came by earlier to get coffee, alone this time. She looked like she'd been crying most of the night, trying to hide it, but not quite pulling it off."

Hope paused. "Did she say anything?"

Ruby shook her head. "But she sat by the window with her hands wrapped around the mug like it was the only warm thing in her life."

Hope looked at the wrapped loaf. "You want to take it to her?"

Ruby nodded. "If that's okay."

Hope paused. "Do you want me to come with you?"

"No," Ruby said gently. "I think it'll mean more if it comes from someone who isn't a grown-up wanting to ask questions."

***

Ruby stood at the weathered gate, loaf tucked under her arm. The small house was quiet. No toys in the yard today. The curtains half-drawn.

She knocked once, then again.

Nova answered, looking surprised. Her eyes were puffy, and she wore a jumper far too big for her frame.

"Hey," Ruby said, shifting the loaf in her arms. "I made this. Thought you might like something warm."

She held out the wrapped loaf.

Nova took it slowly, like it might disappear. Her hands trembled just slightly.

"I'm not very good at talking," Ruby added. "But … I know what it's like to need kindness and not know how to ask for it."

Nova blinked fast, swallowing. "Thank you."

Ruby gave a small nod. "It's Anna's recipe. She was Joe's wife. It says, 'always give one away.' So, that's what I'm doing."

Nova gave a fragile smile. "That's a good kind of instruction."

Ruby smiled and turned to leave quietly the way she'd come, as Nova gently shut the door.

***

Later that afternoon, Hope found a folded note tucked under the café front mat.

Thank you. It reminded me what safe tastes like. Nova.

Hope tucked the note into the back of Anna's recipe book, pressing it between the pages like a flower.

CHAPTER 11

The café was dark, save for the soft pool of light over the counter where Hope was putting away clean coffee mugs. She'd stayed up late restocking dwindling cake supplies. The air still smelled of lemon and cinnamon, the kind of scents that linger. Just as she was reaching to turn off the lamp, a hesitant knock sounded at the back door.

Hope blinked. This time of night?

She opened it cautiously, her breath catching. Nova stood on the step, her face pale and drawn. In her arms, Lily clutched a small bundle wrapped in a tartan blanket. The blanket twitched, and a soft whimper followed.

"Hope," Nova's voice cracked. "I'm so sorry. Daisy … she's hurt."

Hope looked down at the bundle. Lily was crying silently, her small fingers gripping the blanket tight around the little dog's trembling body.

"Come in," Hope said at once, stepping back. "Come in, love."

Inside, Lily laid Daisy carefully on a clean tea towel spread over the café table. The dachshund whimpered again, her tiny body rigid with pain. Hope crouched beside her, heart sinking as she gently stroked the dog's ear.

"What happened?" she asked, glancing up.

Nova didn't answer at first. Her arms were wrapped tightly around herself, as if she were holding something in.

"It was an accident," she said finally, voice small. "Evan just … he lost his temper. She got underfoot."

"He kicked her," Lily burst out suddenly, voice high and shaking. "He did it on purpose, Mum! He was yelling and …"

Nova's eyes flooded. "Lily, that's enough."

"No," Hope said gently, standing now. "No, sweetheart. Thank you for telling me."

Lily dropped her head, one hand still on Daisy's blanket.

Hope kept her voice calm and steady. "We need to get her to Joe. I'll call him now on his after-hours number."

Joe answered after two rings, voice thick with sleep, but sharpening once Hope explained.

"Bring her in. I'll meet you at the clinic."

Hope hung up and turned to Nova. "Can you ride with me? Or do you need a moment?"

Nova shook her head, tears glinting. "No. I … I'll come."

The drive was quiet, broken only by Daisy's soft whimpers and Lily's occasional sniffle from the backseat. Hope kept her hands steady on the wheel. Nova stared out the window, her face turned to the dark hills beyond.

"I know this isn't easy," Hope said quietly, "but this … this isn't nothing, Nova. A man who'll hurt a dog …"

"I know," Nova whispered. "I didn't think he'd ever hurt anyone who was a lot smaller than him."

Hope didn't press, just let the words settle. "You don't have to go back tonight. You and Lily can stay at my cottage."

Nova let out a breath like she hadn't realised she'd been holding it.

***

Joe was waiting at the clinic door, pulling on a jumper and rubbing sleep from his eyes. He nodded at them, all business now.

"Let's take a look at her."

Inside, under the examination light, Daisy trembled as Joe examined her leg with tender fingers. He worked in silence, frowning slightly.

"Fracture's likely," he said eventually. "She's in pain. I'll keep her tonight, get her on fluids and something for the pain and swelling. X-rays in the morning."

Lily's face crumpled again. Joe crouched beside her and offered a soft smile. "She's a brave little dog. You did the right thing bringing her."

Nova nodded but didn't speak. Her hands were clenched in her lap.

Joe glanced at Hope and tilted his head toward the hallway. She followed, out of Lily's earshot.

"Are they safe?" he asked quietly.

Hope shook her head. "No. They're not going back. I'll take them home with me tonight."

Joe's jaw tensed. He looked like he wanted to say more but held it back. "All right. I'll call you in the morning."

Back at the cottage, Hope laid out clean towels and one of her T-shirts for Nova and Lily. The spare room was small and half-filled with boxes, but it was warm. She'd cleared the bed beneath the window to hold both Nova and Lily for the night. Lily was curled up by herself now under the covers, eyes wide and exhausted. Nova sat in a nearby chair, shoulders sagging.

"Thank you," she murmured as Hope handed her a cup of chamomile tea. "I didn't know where else to go."

"You came to the right place," Hope said softly.

Hope knelt and gently tucked the blankets around Lily's small frame, brushing back a wisp of hair. "You were very brave tonight," she whispered.

Lily looked up at her, eyes wet but steady. "He scares Daisy," she said, voice barely above a breath. "And Mum too."

Hope swallowed the ache rising in her throat. She looked to Nova, who blinked fast, then nodded once, silently.

"You should go to the police," Hope said finally, keeping her voice low and even. "What happened tonight, it matters. It's not just about Daisy. Or even about you."

Nova didn't speak.

Hope stood, resting a gentle hand on her shoulder. "It's about Lily too."

Nova stared down at her daughter. After a long moment, she whispered, "I don't want her growing up thinking this is what love looks like."

Hope nodded. "Then let's try something different."

"Not tonight …" Nova trailed off.

Hope softened. "Alright. Let's wait until tomorrow."

***

The morning sun streamed into the cottage kitchen, catching the floating motes of dust in soft gold. Hope moved around the bench, pouring hot water into old, mismatched mugs. Nova sat at the table, hair damp, wearing one of Hope's old flannel shirts. Her fingers traced the rim of her mug, still unsteady.

"She asked if Daisy could come home today," Nova said, her voice low, angling her head towards Lily who was alternating between softly patting Tiger the cat and dragging a piece of wool around the floor for the kitten to chase.

Hope slid a slice of toast onto a plate. "She might need to stay for a few days at the vets. Joe said she's tougher than she looks though. I think she might have that in common with you."

Nova gave a half-smile, but it didn't reach her eyes.

A knock sounded at the back door, soft but certain. Hope startled slightly, wiping her hands on a tea towel. When she opened the door, Joe stood there, wind-ruffled but calm, wearing the quiet steadiness that was becoming strangely familiar.

"Morning," he said gently. "Didn't want to call in case anyone was still sleeping."

"Come in," Hope said, stepping aside.

Joe sat down across from Nova and offered a warm smile. "Daisy had a good night. Just one broken leg bone. She's stiff and bruised, but no internal bleeding. I'd like to keep her just for a few days to monitor things to make sure there is no delayed shock, but Lily can come to visit her this afternoon if that's all right with you."

Nova's eyes shone with sudden relief. "Thank you."

Joe gave a small nod. "You did the right thing by her. Both of you did."

He let the moment settle, then cleared his throat gently. "Nova … I know this might feel like a lot right now. But I wanted to mention someone who might be able to help. Just someone to talk to, no pressure."

Nova looked wary, her fingers tightening around the mug.

"Her name's Eve Harvey," he said. "She's Pastor Tom's wife."

Nova didn't speak, but her brow furrowed.

"She's not pushy," Joe added. "She's … practical and kind. She's helped a few women in town. Quietly."

Hope, leaning against the sink, looked over with interest. "I haven't met her," she admitted slowly. "I've … kept a bit of distance."

Joe looked at her gently. "She's worth meeting. You'd like her, I think."

Hope wasn't sure what to say to that. The term pastor's wife still made something tighten in her chest, a memory of eyes turned away. She'd seen too many people in church clothes be present when things had the appearance of going well, but when there was real conflict or pain, they weren't there. She had been listening carefully though, and Joe's voice held no performance, no pressure, just steady confidence in a woman he clearly respected.

"She doesn't push faith on others?" Hope asked, careful.

Joe shook his head. "She just lives it. That's different."

Nova was quiet for a long moment. Then, very softly, "I don't know if I'm ready to talk. Not properly."

"You don't have to," Joe said. "Sometimes it's just about letting someone sit with you in it."

Hope met Nova's eyes. "I'd be willing to meet her with you. If that helps."

That surprised them both. Maybe Hope most of all. But it felt right. It was time.

Nova gave a small nod, tears welling again. "We could just have a quick chat with her. I don't know what comes next."

Joe stood, brushing his hands on his jeans. "You don't need to. Just listen to some options."

"I have Eve's number inside a book she leant me," Hope said, reaching for her phone. "I'll text her now."

Joe smiled at her then, one of those quiet smiles that said more than words. "I think you'll both find her surprisingly different."

As he stepped out into the sunlight, Hope lingered by the window. She wasn't sure what she believed about God, or churches, or second chances. But maybe people like Eve, and men like Joe, were part of the answer.

***

By mid-afternoon, the café had settled into that familiar hush Hope had come to love. Chairs were neatly pushed back around tables, the counters wiped clean, and the gentle tick of the wall clock filled the space between soft footsteps as they prepared for the evening.

Asha had fallen asleep, curled up with her stuffed toy wombat in the storeroom. Ruby lingered in the kitchen, absentmindedly rinsing mugs and flicking a tea towel over her shoulder like she belonged there. And, Hope supposed, she did.

Ruby glanced over. "Did Nova and Lily leave?"

Hope leaned back against the bench, folding her arms loosely. "They're not going back to Evan."

Ruby looked up at that, eyes sharp with interest. "Seriously?"

Hope nodded. "They're going to stay in the granny flat behind Pastor Tom and Eve's house for a few days. Just while they figure out what comes next."

Ruby raised her eyebrows. "Isn't that like … church central?"

A smile tugged at the corner of Hope's mouth. "That's what I thought."

She picked up a clean mug and turned it slowly. "But today I met Eve. Properly. Joe introduced us."

Ruby leaned an elbow on the sink. "And?"

Hope shrugged lightly. "She's not what I expected."

Ruby waited, sensing more.

"She's warm. No performance. No fixing. She just listened. Offered a cup of tea and a quiet space. She didn't ask Nova a thousand questions. Just made room. For talking, or for silence."

There was a pause. Steam from the kettle curled softly in the air between them.

Hope's voice lowered. "I think I've been holding everyone at arm's length, especially anything that smelled like church. But Eve … she made it feel like maybe genuine faith isn't about unwritten rules and Sunday faces.

Maybe it's people actually being real. Having hands that help, a desire to understand, and hearts that wait to listen."

Ruby didn't say anything right away, but her expression shifted to become something thoughtful, even cautious hopefulness.

"I didn't know you were still open to all that," Ruby said finally, watching her carefully.

"I wasn't sure either," Hope admitted. "But something about Eve challenged me … and I realised that although I didn't feel God's presence in places I ran from, my experience here might be different."

Another pause. Then Ruby asked, quietly, "Do you think Nova will be okay?"

Hope reached out and gently took the tea towel from Ruby's shoulder, folding it. "She's scared. But she's braver than she knows. And she's not alone."

She looked at Ruby then and held her gaze. "Neither are you."

Ruby swallowed and glanced away, but she didn't leave.

Hope didn't push, just stood there in the soft light, letting the truth linger in the air.

Outside, the evening deepened. A prayer formed in Hope's heart. It was just a whisper, asking God to protect Nova and Lily, and to show them a safe way forward. She felt heard.

CHAPTER 12

*R*uby hadn't meant to stay long. She'd come over with a container of leftover muffins from the café and a quick excuse in her back pocket—Hope sent me, just checking in—but Lily had answered the door barefoot and grinning, pulling her inside with paint-smudged fingers.

"We're making signs for Daisy's welcome home!" Lily announced. "Mum says she can come back tomorrow!"

Nova was folding laundry on the couch, still tired but with more colour in her cheeks. She smiled when she saw Ruby.

"Thanks for coming over. Lily would love company, would you like to stay for a bit?"

Ruby hesitated, then nodded. "Sure. For a bit."

She helped Lily hang a sheet of cardboard over the verandah railing, holding it still while she added fingerprints to look like pink paw prints along the bottom edge. The garden behind the granny flat cottage buzzed with bees, fragrant with rosemary and lavender. The sun filtered through gum leaves overhead, and for a moment, everything felt strangely ... peaceful.

"Ruby?" a voice called gently from the gate.

She turned to see a woman walking toward them, carrying a tray with iced tea and lemon slices. Her hair was pulled up loosely, and her cotton maxi dress fluttered in the breeze.

"Hi," she said with a smile. "You must be Ruby. I'm Eve."

There was no judgement in her voice, no analysis, just warmth. The kind that reached beneath Ruby's guard before she could stop it.

"Hi," Ruby said. She wiped her hands on her jeans and looked down. "I didn't mean to intrude or anything."

"You're not," Eve said simply. "If you ever need it, this is your home too."

While Lily continued wrapping the verandah railing with crepe paper streamers, they sat beneath the big gum tree in the yard, the dappled shade falling across the table. Nova had gone inside to answer her phone. Ruby sipped her iced tea in silence, the glass cool in her hands, Eve's presence calm beside her.

"You look like something's on your mind," Eve said eventually, her tone gentle, not accusing.

Ruby didn't respond at first. She watched the condensation bead on her glass, noticed the faint tremble in her hands.

"I haven't talked to anyone about this," she said at last.

Eve didn't interrupt. She just waited.

"I'm pregnant," Ruby said quietly. "And I haven't told anyone … Not Hope. Not the father, he was a brief fling, long gone."

Ruby paused. But Eve didn't speak into the silence. Just gave her an opportunity to continue.

"I haven't figured it all out. I'm not even sure if I want to keep it."

The air felt thinner, like the truth had drawn out all the oxygen. But Eve didn't flinch. She simply reached across and laid a hand over Ruby's. Not to restrain, not to persuade, just to be there.

"Thank you for trusting me," she said softly. "That's a big thing, Ruby. A brave thing to open up about and share."

"I don't feel brave," Ruby whispered.

"Sometimes being brave doesn't feel like it," Eve said. "It just feels like surviving."

Tears stung behind Ruby's eyes. "I keep thinking about what people will say. What Hope will say. She's been so good to me."

"She will still be good to you," Eve said gently. "Maybe even more so, because she'll understand. Love isn't something that disappears when the story gets messy."

Ruby stared down at her lap. "I didn't mean for it to happen."

"That's true for so many young women," Eve replied. "But it doesn't mean God can't bring something beautiful from it. Whatever choice you make … you don't have to do it alone."

The tears spilled then. They were silent, hot, and fast. Ruby swiped at them quickly, but Eve didn't look away. She just passed her a clean hand-kerchief and sat in supportive silence.

***

That afternoon, the little bell above the clinic door gave a soft chime as Ruby stepped inside, hugging her arms across her chest.

The front desk was empty; Joe's receptionist Sarah might have left early today. Ruby could hear the low murmur of a voice in the back and the gentle shuffle of paws on linoleum. The smell of antiseptic, hay, and something faintly herbal drifted through the air. Familiar. Calming.

"Joe?" she called, trying to sound casual.

A moment later, he appeared from behind a door, wiping his hands on a towel. His expression shifted from surprised to warm in an instant.

"Hey there," he said. "You just missed Nova and Lily. They've been visiting Daisy. Lily brought her a homemade dog biscuit and picture she'd drawn her."

Ruby smiled faintly. "That sounds about right."

Joe stepped closer, his eyes scanning hers. "Everything okay?"

She hesitated. "Can we talk? Just ... for a few minutes."

"Of course." He gestured toward the back room. "Come through. It's quiet out the back. There's less tail-wagging, although Bounty's there, slobber and all."

Joe poured her a glass of water and set it on the workbench beside a row of labelled medicine vials. The air was cooler in here, still and private.

Ruby tapped her fingernails on the stainless-steel workbench, unsure how to start. Joe didn't push. He just leaned against the bench across from her, arms folded loosely, waiting.

"You encouraged Nova and Lily to meet with Eve because you knew she was safe."

He nodded.

"I went to visit them this morning. Stayed for a while. Eve was there."

Joe didn't say anything, but his face softened.

"I told her something," Ruby said. Her throat tightened. "And now I think I need to tell someone else. Just to ... say it out loud again. Before I tell Hope."

A beat passed.

"I'm pregnant," she said.

It fell into the silence like a stone into still water. Sudden, heavy, and impossible to take back.

Joe didn't react at first. No sharp intake of breath. No shock. Just a long, slow blink.

"All right," he said gently. "That's a lot to carry on your own."

Ruby looked down at her hands. "I've been scared to tell anyone. I kept thinking if Hope found out, she might send me packing. I don't exactly scream 'responsible adult'."

Joe's voice was low. "You'd be surprised what Hope understands."

"But she's already taken a chance on me. A big one. This could feel like … a betrayal."

He shook his head slowly. "Hope sees people. Not reputations. People."

She swallowed. "What if she doesn't want a pregnant teenager living in the back storeroom of her café?"

"Then she'll find you a proper room. And probably knit you a blanket before the week's out."

That startled a laugh out of Ruby, who knew the knitting was unlikely. Her hand went to her mouth, tears rising quick and hot. She blinked them back.

Joe's voice softened. "You don't seem like a burden, Ruby. Not to me. And I'd wager not to Hope either. She may be tough around the edges, but underneath, she's sewn together with compassion. You already know that."

"I don't even know what I'm going to do yet," Ruby said quietly. "About the baby. About anything."

Joe was quiet for a moment. Then he said, "That's okay. You don't have to have the whole road mapped out. You just need to keep taking a small step forward."

She looked at him then and some of the fear seemed to drain out of her shoulders. "I just didn't want to face it alone," she confessed.

"You won't."

***

The afternoon sun lay warm across the back lawn behind the café, casting long, gentle shadows from the gum trees beyond. Ruby sat on the grass with her knees tucked to her chest, watching a trail of ants marching past. Asha lay sprawled beside her in a patch of sun, ears flicking lazily at the occasional fly.

"You don't care, do you?" Ruby murmured, rubbing behind Asha's ear. "You'd still wag your tail no matter what."

Asha groaned contentedly and nudged her paw against Ruby's leg.

"I'm pregnant," Ruby said quietly. "There. I said it again out loud."

The words hung in the air. Asha didn't blink, just rolled slightly so her belly caught the sun.

"I haven't told Hope yet. I'm scared she'll think I've taken advantage of her. Like she's given me all this and I went and wrecked it."

Ruby swallowed hard, throat tight.

"I don't even know what I'm going to do. Some days I think I could do it. Keep the baby. Start over." She exhaled. "Other days I just want to disappear."

Asha gave a soft grunt and nosed at Ruby's arm like she understood every word.

Behind her, the screen door creaked softly closed. Hope had come to hang out a tea towel and had paused at the doorway, unseen. She'd caught the quiet words, the ache in them, the longing not to be judged. She stepped back without a sound, giving Ruby space, but she took it all in, and the significance. Hope considered the enormity of decisions ahead.

***

The café was quiet now, the last of the chairs turned up, the floor swept, the scent of roasted capsicum and warm bread lingering in the air. Ruby was drying cutlery, moving slower than usual, eyes shadowed with thought.

Hope moved behind the counter, folding a clean cloth. "Nice night," she said casually. "Asha seems content out back."

Ruby nodded. "She's a good listener."

Hope glanced at her. "I heard a little of what you said to Asha earlier. I wasn't eavesdropping, I just stepped out to hang up a tea towel."

Ruby froze; shoulders tense.

Hope set the cloth down and moved slowly around the counter. "I heard you mention the baby."

Ruby looked away, blinking fast. "I was going to tell you. I just … didn't know how."

Hope sat on the edge of the bench, folding her hands. "I imagine it took a lot just to say it out loud at all."

Ruby's lip trembled. "You've done so much for me already. I thought … maybe this would be too much."

Hope reached over gently and brushed a strand of hair behind Ruby's ear. "You're not a project, Ruby. You're not some broken thing I took in out of charity." She paused, her voice soft and steady. "You matter. With mistakes, and questions, and scary news you don't know what to do with."

Tears spilled silently down Ruby's cheeks. "I don't know if I can do this."

"You don't have to have the answer tonight," Hope said. "You just need to know you're not alone."

For a long moment, neither of them spoke. The quiet hum of the fridge and the tick of the wall clock filled the space like a gentle heartbeat.

Then Ruby whispered, "You're not going to kick me out?"

Hope gave a small, incredulous smile. "I'm going to make you some ginger and lemongrass tea. That's what I'm going to do."

Ruby laughed, a surprised sound. Hope pulled her into a hug, firm and steady.

"You're not alone in this, Ruby. Not now. Not ever."

CHAPTER 13

The late afternoon sun filtered through the gums, dappled light flickering across the path. It had been a dry summer, but last week's showers in the Highlands had sent enough water down for the river to flow well again, carrying life into the valley.

Hope had closed the café early today, sensing that both she and Ruby were running on fumes after the week they'd had. Ruby was off learning how to crochet at Nova's, and Hope had accepted Joe's invitation to walk along the riverbank. He'd mentioned platypus spotting, though he hadn't brought binoculars or mentioned any real plan. Perhaps they both just needed to get outside.

Hope stuffed her hands deep into her jacket pockets. The quiet between them wasn't awkward, just full. Solid. Like shared ground they didn't have to name.

Joe walked beside her, close enough to hear her breath but not to crowd her personal space. He kicked at a stone and watched it skitter ahead like a thought he hadn't yet found the words for.

"You okay?" Hope asked after a while.

He drew a breath, shrugged. "Just thinking."

"About Ruby?"

He nodded. "And Nova. And … other things."

She didn't press. Just let the sounds of the water and the rustle of gums fill the silence.

They reached a bend in the trail where the trees opened wide, light spilling through like grace. Joe stopped, arms folded, gaze fixed on the river.

"You know, when Anna and I were trying for a baby ... we didn't tell anyone. Thought we'd surprise our folks at the twelve-week mark."

Hope turned toward him, breath catching.

"We never made it that far," he said. "Anna miscarried just before three months. A week later, after some tests, we got the cancer diagnosis."

A long silence settled. The river gurgled over a cluster of rocks.

"I'm so sorry," Hope said softly. "You've never mentioned ..."

He shook his head. "It all blurred together. Grief on top of grief. Like standing in the surf and getting hit by one wave, and then another before you can breathe again."

Hope reached out, her hand brushing his. When he didn't pull away, she let her fingers settle gently into his.

"I remember sitting with her," he said, voice low. "Thinking how unfair it was, that she never got to hold our baby. And then ... never got the chance to grow old, either. I buried both of those dreams in the same year."

Tears stung Hope's eyes, but she blinked them back.

"I guess seeing Ruby... it just hit something old. And Nova, running from what she thought was love—it made me realise how lucky I was. Even with how it ended. Anna loved me. We were safe. That's more than a lot of people get."

Hope gave his hand a soft squeeze. "I'm sorry, Joe."

He looked at her then. "Me too. But it helps. Talking."

Their hands drifted apart, and they walked on in silence, steps falling into an easy rhythm.

"I think Ruby needs someone steady," Hope said after a moment. "Someone who won't run or push her too hard."

"She's got that," Joe replied. "In you."

Hope gave a half-laugh. "Sometimes, I don't know what I'm doing."

"That's how I know you're the right person for the job," he said, deadpan. She gave him a look, and he grinned.

The trail dipped toward a calm bend in the river, where the water ran deep and glassy. Joe stooped and picked up a flat stone and flicked it across the surface. It skipped three times before vanishing with a soft plunk.

Hope found her own stone, smaller and not as smooth. She flung it without any skill. It made one sad skip and flopped.

Joe raised a brow. "Respectable effort."

"You patronise me beautifully," she said.

"I've had practice. Craig's boys used to throw rocks like wounded ducks."

She laughed.

They lingered a moment, watching a pair of galahs chase each other in the treetops, their bellies catching the light.

Hope nudged him with her elbow. "Have you ever actually seen a platypus here?"

Joe shook his head. "Not once."

"Then what's the point of coming all the way out here?"

"Hope," he said solemnly, "platypus watching is about the possibility. It's a metaphor."

"For what?"

He looked out along the riverbank. "For how life sometimes gives you small, miraculous things if you stand still long enough."

She gave him a look. "That's suspiciously poetic for someone who once stitched up a cow with a biro."

"I'm multi-talented," he said, shrugging.

Hope's smile reached her eyes.

They stood like that for a while. Beside the impossible river, waiting for a miracle.

Then Hope realised that, after the past few years she'd survived, just being here with Joe, feeling safe, seemed like one.

After a few minutes of listening to the river gurgle as it slipped past them, Joe turned and looked at Hope. Her brow was now furrowed, her eyes distant, deep in thought.

"You don't have to talk. But if something's on your mind ..." he said.

Hope hesitated, staring into the river before her.

"It's not just what happened with Nova or Ruby," she said eventually. "It's me too. Lately, I've been ... struggling."

Joe turned toward her but didn't speak. He just listened.

"When I was with Mark," she said slowly, "I was in survival mode. Constantly second-guessing, trying to keep things calm, to not set him off. I didn't realise how much that did to me ... until after I left."

She drew in a shaky breath. "It's strange. You'd think it would get easier, being out. But sometimes I feel like the war is still going inside me. I've had a few panic attacks. Out of nowhere. I'll be in the storeroom or the shower or closing at night, and suddenly I can't breathe. My chest tightens, like something terrible's just about to happen."

Joe didn't speak, but the quiet between them felt safe.

"I guess I thought once I was free, I'd feel free," she said, letting out a breath that was almost a laugh, but not quite. "But it's messier than that. I still worry. That he'll come back. Or that I'll let someone else in and not see the signs. That I'll miss it ... until it's too late."

Joe's brow furrowed with quiet empathy. "That's *not* nothing, Hope."

"I know." Her voice wavered. "I try to keep it together. For Ruby, for the café, for ... everyone. But some days, I'm just managing."

Joe reached out, brushing his fingers lightly over hers. "You don't have to manage it alone."

Hope looked at him then, her expression searching.

"You're not scared off by all this?"

"Not even close."

She gave a small, shaky smile.

"I think you're one of the bravest people I know," he added.

Joe's words hung in the dusk, quiet and solid.

She swallowed hard, blinking fast. "I really needed to hear that."

He squeezed her hand. "Then I'm glad I said it."

The last of the sunlight began to fade, and they turned to start walking back along the trail.

***

The sun was setting by the time they reached the back path to Hope's cottage, brushing the sky in soft lavender and muted peach. Hope opened the gate, and Asha bounded out to greet them, tail wagging, tongue lolling, eyes shining with the kind of uncomplicated joy only dogs can manage.

She sniffed them both in turn, satisfied they were hers, then trotted up to the porch.

Joe paused at the steps. "I should head home. Let you get some rest."

Hope nodded, though part of her didn't want him to go. "Thanks for walking with me."

"Anytime."

She watched as he made his way down the drive, his silhouette long and steady in the dusk. Only when the sound of his car had faded did she head inside.

The cottage was quiet, still holding the warmth of the day. Hope hung up her coat near the door and stepped forward into the living room. And stopped.

Curled together on the armchair near the window were Tiger and the ginger kitten, whom she'd never quite named properly. They slept in a tangle of fur and whiskers, purring in soft harmony. Tiger, ever patient and gentle, had accepted the nervous, wide-eyed rescue without fuss. And now here they were, chest to chest, breathing in sync like they'd always belonged together.

Hope sank slowly onto the couch, watching them with a tightness in her chest. The kitten—Ginger, she now decided—had come from a place of fear and hunger, skittish and unsure. But over time, through Tiger's quiet and steady presence, she had learned to rest.

To trust.

To curl up and purr.

Hope let the thought settle.

Maybe this was what healing looked like. Not some thunderclap moment of transformation. But a slow, steady return. A walking beside someone safe until your heart remembered how to breathe again.

She exhaled and closed her eyes for a moment, letting the quiet wrap around her.

Could grace look like this too?

Could God be the one who walked beside you, gently waiting and never forcing, just holding out what you couldn't quite take yet?

She opened her eyes to the sleeping animals.

Their purring sounded like a lullaby.

Tonight, no fear clawed at her edges. She felt safe.

CHAPTER 14

The café was quiet in the fading light. It was the kind of hush that usually signalled the end of a day, not the possibility of a beginning.

Hope moved slowly through the café, placing a jug of wildflowers in the centre of the circle of chairs she'd arranged near the fireplace. She'd chosen her softest lighting, turning on the fairy lights looped on the rafters, and placing a few flickering tea lights in old china cups on the tables. The air smelled of spice, and honey cake.

Monday was usually her catch-up day, involving prep, paperwork, and ordering. But when Eve had gently asked whether the women's support group she'd been leading could meet here this evening, explaining it was a quiet gathering for women learning to rebuild after abusive relationships, Hope had felt challenged to open the door. The café had become a kind of haven lately, not just for customers, but for her too.

Eve had acknowledged that churches didn't always know how to help women coming from painful places. She had spoken to Hope about years of walking alongside women through court dates and counselling. Her motivation to help came with experience and understanding.

Still, Hope had told herself she'd just host. Set up. Keep the kettle warm. Nothing more.

She left one chair slightly outside the circle … her own.

Just before seven, the first women began to arrive. Nova came in quietly after dropping Lily off to spend the evening with Ruby at Hope's cottage. This was her first time being invited into the circle as well. Her steps were slow but determined. A younger woman Hope didn't know followed, pushing a stroller with a sleeping baby, eyes rimmed with tiredness. Two others came in laughing softly, their voices low and tentative.

Eve was last. She moved through the room greeting each woman with a gentle smile, a touch on the shoulder, and a word of welcome. When she reached Hope, she simply said, "Thank you. This place already feels so inviting."

Hope gave a small smile. "I've put the kettle on and there's a range of herbal teas and coffee available."

"That's more than enough."

The women settled into the circle, tea in hand, a plate of Hope's sliced honey cake on the table between them. Hope stayed behind the counter, wiping down a spotless surface just to keep her hands busy.

Eve began, her voice calm and steady. "Some of you know each other. Some are new. But tonight, this is our space. There's no pressure. No need to perform or pretend. You can just ... be."

She spoke to clarify. "As you know, this isn't a Bible Study group. It's a space to remember who you really are. However, I know many of you do have a faith background. So, this evening, I want to remind you that God sees you. He cares about you. His love is different to what many of you have known."

She opened her Bible.

"Jesus says in the book of Matthew that He is ... *'gentle and humble in heart.'*"

Eve let the words linger in the quiet.

"God understands your story," she said softly. "He is the Creator of the Universe. He's all-powerful, but … He is also gentle. He is humble, and He is safe."

"Hearing this might fill us with uncertainty," Eve said, "because some of us never experienced safety in relationships and the idea of being in a relationship with anyone again, even God, might make you feel unsure."

"I want us to sit with this verse. Not with fear, but with longing. What would it have meant to be in a safe relationship? What would it feel like to know a love that protects? A love that is caring. A love that never demands you become small. That allows you to feel safe?"

Iris, an older woman in the group, said, "For years I thought if I kept the house perfect, if I smiled enough, he'd stop calling me names. But it didn't work. I realise now, I wasn't being loved. I was being controlled."

Jess, the younger woman with the baby, breathed in deeply before saying, "I grew up in a home with violence, so I thought relationships all happened with conflict. That passion meant raised voices and abusive language. It never felt safe. Never peaceful."

Eve waited for a few moments of silence before speaking again. "So, what does love look like, if it's not what we have known? The Bible says in 1 Corinthians that, '*Love is patient, love is kind … it is not easily angered.*' That's God's design for love. Not love that scares us. Not love that confuses or bruises. Love that is safe."

Hope stood listening and thinking about Mark's indifferent silence when she cried after he shook her. The way he would brush past her like she was furniture. The quiet threats. The words that still echoed. And how long it took her to believe she wasn't the problem. She wasn't ready to speak. But something in her eased. Slowly, she stepped forward and took an empty seat in the circle.

***

Later, Eve read the Bible again, Luke 12:7. "*The very hairs on your head are all numbered. Don't be afraid; you are worth more than many sparrows.*"

Eve let the words settle in the warm silence before continuing, "If you have ever been called too much, too loud, too weak, too slow … I want you to hear this: God knows you. And He thinks you are valuable."

After the women had a moment to let this sink in, Eve invited them to speak. "If you feel ready, I'd love you to share … what names have stuck to you in the past? And what names might God be offering you now?"

Jess spoke softly into the group. "My ex used to call me 'damaged goods.' Said no one else would want me. For a long time, I believed him."

Eve leaned forward gently. "What name do you think God might be whispering to you?"

Jess hesitated. Then, almost in a whisper, "Maybe … wanted."

Nova then spoke up, her voice shaking with emotion. "After I escaped, I kept calling myself a fool. A failure. But I'm learning that I was brave. I didn't fail; I survived."

Eve smiled at Nova warmly. "That's right. You are not your shame. You are not your scars. You are brave."

Hope didn't speak, but the words struck something deep: *you are not your scars.*

Eve spoke gently. "Many of you have lost parts of yourself in damaging relationships. I wonder if you can share some of these things tonight …"

Nova, who had mostly been quiet, spoke again. "My confidence. That's what he took. I walk into rooms and shrink, like I'm not supposed to be there. I want to stop apologising for breathing."

Someone else murmured, "I miss laughing."

Hope felt compelled to speak. She looked down at her hands, then up at the circle. "I used to think surviving was enough," she said, voice quiet. "Since leaving, I've thought if I can just make it through the day without a panic attack, I'd won. But lately I've realised … I'm tired of holding my breath. I want to learn how to exhale again. I want to feel peace and joy."

There was a pause, then someone whispered, "Me too."

***

As the evening drew to a close, Eve brought out a shallow bowl filled with smooth river stones and passed it around the circle.

"You don't have to take one," she said. "But if it helps, these are a reminder. That healing takes time, and that the hard places in life you've survived have actually shaped you into something strong and beautiful, even when you feel worn thin."

Each woman took a stone.

Hope rolled hers in her palm. It was cool and grounding, its weight oddly reassuring.

Eve lifted a cup filled with metallic ink markers. "If you feel ready, I invite you to write a word on your stone. Just one. A name you sense God might be speaking over you. Something true. Something healing. You can take it home and keep it visible. Let it remind you of who you really are."

The women each selected a marker. One wrote "*Free*". Another, "*Seen*". A third, with trembling fingers, carefully wrote "*Whole*".

Hope waited.

Watching them, she felt unsure. It felt too intimate, too exposing. So simple, but so weighty.

The silver pen hovered in her hand.

A word came. Unexpected. But steady. "*Treasured.*"

Not looked down upon.

Not just tolerated.

Valuable.

Wanted. Loved because she existed. Not for what she did or didn't do.

Her throat tightened. She pressed the pen down and slowly wrote the word, her hand steadying as she shaped each letter.

Eve prayed simply for the group as they closed the evening. Hope just listened, feeling a quiet sense of joy.

The women stood and thanked Hope for opening the café for them, then drifted out into the night.

After the others had gone, Eve stayed behind to help carry mugs and plates to the kitchen.

"Thank you again," she said gently to Hope.

"I didn't plan to … share anything," Hope admitted.

Eve smiled. "You didn't just offer us a space tonight, Hope. You made room, for others and for yourself."

Hope stood in the doorway as Eve left. Moonlight spilled across the floor behind her, soft and steady.

Tonight, for the first time in a long while, she didn't feel like she was standing outside the circle.

***

Later that evening, Hope placed the stone on her bedside table.

She didn't fall asleep feeling alone.

She felt seen.

She felt treasured.

CHAPTER 15

The first crack of thunder split the air just as they were setting up for evening customers.

Hope was outside in the café's garden, clipping basil and rosemary, when the sky above Wombat Valley shifted from powder blue to apricot, tinged with bruised grey clouds. A strange, electric stillness settled over the air. It was the kind of feeling that makes the hair stand on the back of your neck.

She looked up. Clouds were building fast, too fast. The kind of storm that didn't bring relief, just tension and trouble.

Inside, Ruby glanced nervously out the window. "That doesn't look friendly."

Hope grabbed a flashlight from under the counter. "Storms like this come fast and loud. I don't think we will have many customers tonight."

Ruby moved towards the back yard, "We should pull in the outdoor timber chairs. This kind of storm can start fires."

Hope gave a tight smile, going out to join her. "That's what I'm afraid of."

A dry wind whipped over chairs and slammed the back door of the café. Ruby and Hope ran around stacking the chairs near the wall.

Asha padded out beside them, tail down, nose lifted, ears twitching at a sound only she could hear.

"You feel that too, girl?" Hope murmured.

Asha let out a low whine.

Then it came, a crack like a tree splitting in half. Hope flinched. A white-hot fork of lightning struck up near the ridge, it looked like a snake striking its prey.

There was no rain. Just a silence that felt too big.

Then the wind gusts began to increase.

Hope caught the smell before she saw it. Burning eucalyptus bark, faint at first, then unmistakable.

Both had just come back inside and Hope was boiling the kettle when the phone buzzed.

Joe Butler.

She answered quickly. "Hey."

"Are you seeing this sky?" he asked, voice clipped. "There's been a dry lightning strike near the entrance to the National Park, it's been fanned into flames. The Rural Fire Service's just been called out. If this westerly wind keeps blowing, Wombat Valley could be directly in the fire's path."

Hope's stomach dropped. The Lyrebird National Park was only fifteen kilometres away.

"Do I need to evacuate?"

"Not yet. It's heading towards the southern end of the valley; you should be safe north of the bridge amongst all the paddocks. I'll call you if anything changes."

A minute later, Hope saw Edith's husband Rob drive past with their son Craig, pulling on their RFS jackets, faces grim.

***

By nightfall, the café lights glowed like a beacon across the bridge. The smoke had thickened, drifting low along the far side of the valley, and Hope had pulled every spare chair, cushion and blanket she could find from her cottage into the café.

Out the front near the road, Ruby had positioned the chalk board that read,

'Community Support Station –
Free Tea, Soup, and Shelter.'

Hope had pulled out the urn, which was now boiling. They had defrosted all their frozen supplies of soup, and the smell of vegetables warmed the air. Ruby stood beside her, slicing sourdough loaves with focused concentration. She hadn't said much, but her eyes darted toward the door every time it creaked open.

The first to arrive was a retired couple from the fire line near Ridge Road. Their hands trembled as they sat, still smelling of smoke and shock. "We didn't think it would come so fast," the woman whispered.

Then came a young mum and her two children, their eyes wide, their car covered in clumps of ash. The little girl clutched a stuffed toy kitten with frayed fur. Hope led them gently toward a table near the back with water and tumblers in the centre. Ruby offered to make the children hot chocolate with marshmallows.

A teenager arrived next, no more than fifteen, with a cattle dog on a lead. He had a look in his eyes that said he'd left behind something that mattered. He didn't speak. Just sat and accepted the sweet hot tea Ruby brought him without meeting her gaze. His boots were caked with ash, one untied. He sat hunched, like he was trying to shrink inside his flannel shirt.

Hope didn't ask questions. She just kept moving by ladling soup, offering damp hand towels, and putting blankets over cold shoulders. Ruby lit a few candles when the power flickered, their soft glow pooling in corners like hush.

No one said much, but the silence was like a living thing, a held breath. They were safe here. Just for now.

Ruby came up behind her at one point and whispered, "You think more will come?"

Hope glanced toward the door.

"I think some already have," she said quietly, and turned back to the soup.

***

Hours later, when the soup pots were empty and children were curled up sleeping in blankets on the floor, Rob and Craig opened the door of the café.

"It's done some damage to houses, but the fire's now under control."

Hope and everyone listening in the café breathed a collective sigh of relief.

"Thanks, Craig. Was anyone hurt?"

"No one was injured." He collapsed in a nearby chair. "But we couldn't save Row's place. It's right outside the National Park and was the first place the fire reached."

Murmurs of conversation whispered around the room. People pulled out mobile phones to call loved ones who had been fighting the fire to check where they were.

Ruby handed both Rob and Craig bottles of water as they rested for a moment near the doorway looking exhausted.

After midnight, Pastor Tom phoned Hope to confirm that they had sounded the all-clear for families to return to their homes. Soon, the gathered tables of townsfolk started to trickle outside to their cars to see whether their yards and outbuildings at home had suffered any damage.

***

The next morning broke soft and grey, with sunshine veiled behind smoke and mist. The wind had calmed, but the air still carried the scorched tang of eucalyptus and earth. Hope stood barefoot at the café's back door, and watched the valley hold its breath.

There was ash on the tables out the back, and as she walked around the front of the café, she saw a scattering of footprints in ash across the verandah where people had come and gone through the night. A couple of blankets were bundled near the door. Someone had scribbled a thank-you note on the back of a napkin and tucked it under the door mat.

Hope stepped out into the yard, the gravel damp with dew, Asha padding beside her.

She turned slowly, taking it all in … the café still standing, the paddocks untouched, the bridge unburnt.

She let out a long breath. "*Thank You,*" she whispered, the words carried on the quiet like smoke drifting upward. It wasn't a fancy prayer. Just the truth.

Inside, Ruby was helping fold blankets. Her eyes looked tired but calm. They shared a glance, not quite a smile, but something close. Hope made a coffee, and Ruby went back to folding.

Then came the crunch of tyres on gravel.

Joe's ute pulled in, streaked with dust and ash. He stepped out slowly, stiff from too many hours on the fireground. His face was drawn, eyes shadowed. But when he saw her in the doorway, he smiled.

Hope came out and met him halfway.

"You survived," she said, and felt her voice catch just slightly.

"Who's going to keep bringing you strays if I didn't?" Joe joked softly.

She handed him a mug of coffee, already prepared but untouched, as if she'd been waiting for him.

Joe looked around, "You kept the lights on all night."

"Seemed the thing to do."

He took the mug and wrapped both hands around it. "This is what real community looks like, Hope. People notice gestures of kindness and they are grateful."

She didn't respond right away. Just looked at him as he sipped the comforting brew, at the soot on his collar, and the tenderness in his gaze. Something inside her shifted. Nothing grand. Just the quiet knowing that his return mattered. More than she'd let herself believe.

"Thank you," she said.

"For what?"

"For coming back safely."

Joe met her eyes, and something passed between them. Not a promise. Not yet.

He handed her back the empty mug with a smile.

"I better head home for a shower and quick sleep before the patients arrive."

Hope looked at him quizzically.

"More animals than people will need saving today." Joe's voice held emotion.

"Let me know if Ruby or I can help in any way."

Joe nodded, giving her a playful salute before turning to hop back into his ute.

**

That afternoon, the church office still carried the faint scent of smoke. It clung to the old carpet and nestled in the folds of Pastor Tom's RFS jacket, draped over the back of his chair. Through the vestry door, sunlight lit the stained glass in quiet colours, spilling pink and gold across his desk.

Tom leaned forward, pen in hand, a small card resting on his desk. He'd drafted and rewritten the first line three times already.

Dear Hope,

I just wanted to thank you …

He paused. That wasn't quite it. This wasn't about politeness. This was about something deeper. She had provided a flicker of light in the dark. The café hadn't just offered soup and shelter. It had opened its arms and offered a safe space.

He tried again.

Hope,

You kept the lights on. Not just in the café, but in people's hearts during a dark night of fear.

Thank you for what you gave so freely, and for holding steady when others needed somewhere to land.

I believe what you did was an act of grace to this town, maybe more than you know. God was working through you to serve others.

With gratitude,

Tom Harvey

He sat back and let the words rest.

Eve stepped into the doorway, setting down a plate of scones beside him.

"I thought you might need a little energy," she said.

Tom smiled. "I'm writing to Hope."

Eve sat opposite him, brushing flour off her hands. "I've been thinking about her. Something's changing."

Tom nodded slowly. "She might not know it yet. But I think she's already taking steps towards finding her way home."

He slid the card into an envelope and sealed it. Not a sermon. Not an invitation. Just truth, quietly given.

***

By mid-afternoon, all the dishes were washed, the blankets packed away, and the urn drained for the last time. Ruby had gone for a walk with Asha, and the quiet felt deep and honest.

Hope sat at the small writing desk in her cottage. A steaming mug of tea sat beside her, and her grandmother's worn Bible lay open. A faded crocheted bookmark had been wedged at the start of 1 John.

After the events of the night before, Hope had felt drawn to open it. Her eyes fell on a verse underlined in her grandmother's careful hand:

"*This is how we know what love is: Jesus Christ laid down his life for us.*" 1 John 3:16.

Hope traced the words with her fingertip. Her throat thickened.

She opened her journal. And wrote –

"*Saved.*"

Hope looked out the window for quite a while, then kept writing.

"*Thank You. For laying Yourself down … and for coming back. For me.*"

CHAPTER 16

The gravel crunched beneath the tyres as Eve's old four-wheel drive rolled to a stop outside what had, only days before, been Rowena's home. Now, only a heap of charred timbers remained, framed by the scorched hillside.

Hope stepped out first, her boots sinking slightly into the damp, ash-softened ground. The air still smelled of smoke … and something more. Loss.

Rowena stood near the edge of what had been her large market vegetable garden, her arms folded tightly across her chest, soot on her cheeks like war paint. A scorched wheelbarrow lay on its side nearby; the front wheel melted into the earth. A few half-burnt pumpkins clung stubbornly to a scorched vine.

Eve hesitated, then walked over slowly.

"Row," she said gently.

Rowena turned. Her eyes were red-rimmed, but her voice was steady. "You came."

"Of course we did," Eve said. Behind her, Hope and Nova were unloading bottled water, gloves, and a container of sandwiches from the back of the four-wheel drive.

Rowena looked past them at her blackened garden beds, and the remains of her building that had served as a cooking school and commercial kitchen.

"I don't even know where to start. I feel like I've lost … not just the house. This was my work. My purpose."

Hope nodded, brushing a strand of hair from her face. "It wasn't just a garden. You fed people from here."

Rowena gave a brittle half-laugh. "And now, after what seemed like a lifetime of building something up, I've got nothing but dirt and charcoal to show for it."

There was a beat of silence.

Then Nova came over with a bucket and a rake. "We thought we could help clear through the debris. Maybe salvage some equipment."

Rowena looked at her, then at Eve who was standing over near where the gardening shed had been, looking at a pile of blackened gardening tools. A moment passed. She exhaled, her shoulders sinking. "Alright. Although the insurance might reimburse me for some of what was built here over the years, I don't know if I have the energy anymore to rebuild or reclaim what has been lost."

The women together stood in respectful quiet, absorbing the truth and pain in what Rowena had said. Acknowledging that the loss for her was incredible.

Eve crouched down and picked up a pitchfork and a shovel, that although black, still looked useful. She carried them over to put near the four-wheel drive.

The movement encouraged the other women to step forward. They worked slowly and carefully. Charred timbers were carefully stepped over, and any salvageable items were gently picked up and inspected. It was quiet work, broken only by the rustle of gloves or the clink of glass. At one point, Rowena bent down and picked up a melted cake tin. She stared at it, unmoving, until Eve gently took it from her and set it aside.

Later, they sat under the only surviving tree. Its leaves were browned but intact. Hope offered Rowena a cup of tea from the thermos.

Hope broke the silence. "I've been thinking," she began. "I want to build up the café menu for winter. By starting to include a variety of soups and warm salads, food that comforts and restores. This will nourish those who'd like something warm to eat other than woodfired pizza. But I can't do all this cooking alone."

Rowena blinked at her. "Hope …"

"I mean it," Hope said quietly. "You have a gift. People come alive around your food. And right now, you need a kitchen. I've got one."

Rowena looked down at her hands, still streaked with ash. "I don't know if I have the emotional energy to start again."

"Start with one pot of soup," Hope said, her tone warm but steady. "Then we can see how you're feeling."

Rowena didn't answer straight away. A breeze stirred the edges of her scarf.

"You'd really let me share your kitchen?" she asked at last.

"I'd be lucky to have you," Hope said. "Besides, you'd be doing me a favour."

Rowena gave a slow nod. Something in her face softened, not quite a smile, but the first breath of one.

From a little distance away, Eve called out, "Row, would you be open to staying in Edith's old cottage for now? It's empty but sturdy. Bit dusty, but it'll keep you warm."

Rowena turned, surprised. "I … couldn't impose."

"You're not," Eve said. "She offered."

Rowena looked from Eve to Hope, then to Nova, who was feeding a sandwich crust to a curious magpie. She pressed a hand to the top of her chest holding back emotions. "I don't know what I did to deserve all this kindness."

Hope touched her arm. "It's not about deserving. It's about showing kindness to others when others have shown it to us."

Rowena nodded, then looked up at the tree's scorched leaves. "Alright then," she said quietly. "Let's see where one pot of soup leads."

***

By the time Hope arrived back at the café, it was just after lunchtime. The smell of smoke still clung faintly to her jumper and hair, and her body ached from lifting and crouching and simply holding space for someone else's grief.

She walked up the driveway and into the back garden, thinking about what jobs she needed to get done this afternoon. The café was closed today, their rest day, and it was blessedly still.

But as she stepped inside through the café back door and looked into the storeroom-turned-bedroom, she saw Ruby sitting on the bed with her knees drawn up, one hand pressed lightly to her lower belly. Her brows were pinched in worry. Beside her, Asha lay, alert watching.

Hope dropped her keys quietly onto the bench. "Hey love. Are you alright?"

Ruby startled, then tried to sit up straighter. "Yeah. Just tired."

Hope stepped closer, crouching a little to meet her eye. "You were holding your stomach. Is it hurting?"

Ruby hesitated. "Sort of. Not bad. Just crampy. Like, pulling. It's been like that on and off."

Hope's concern sharpened. "Have you had any appointments yet? Since you found out?"

Ruby shook her head, eyes flicking away. "I just did a home test. That's it."

"No doctor, no blood test, no ultrasound?"

Another shake of her head. "I didn't want to deal with it yet."

Hope sat down beside her slowly. "Ruby, you don't have to make any big decisions today. But we do need to make sure you're okay. And we need to know how far along you are."

Ruby looked down at her hands. "What if I go and they're judging or pressuring me?"

Hope's voice was steady. "Then we walk out. But I know the doctor at the Wombat Valley surgery. She's gentle, and kind. She'll look after you. I'll come with you the whole way."

Ruby gave a slow nod, uncertain but not resistant.

Hope smiled gently. "Let's call and see if they can squeeze you in this afternoon, if not, we'll go first thing in the morning. Deal?"

"Deal," Ruby murmured.

Hope stood and reached for her phone. "One step at a time, alright? That's how we do this."

She glanced out the kitchen window. Smoke still hung in the hills, but the sky was starting to clear. She rested her hand on the windowsill, silently praying.

Lord, give me strength. For Row. For Ruby. For whatever comes next.

Hope stepped into the café kitchen and pulled out her phone, the weight of worry sitting quietly beneath her ribs. She scrolled to the number for the Wombat Valley Surgery and pressed call.

After a few rings, a familiar voice answered. "Wombat Valley Surgery, this is Natalie."

"Hi, Natalie, it's Hope Elkins. I was wondering if we could get an appointment this afternoon, or tomorrow, for a young woman in my care. She's pregnant and has been experiencing some cramping."

There was a pause on the other end, then Natalie's voice softened. "Oh, right. Thanks for ringing. How far along is she?"

"We're not sure," Hope admitted. "She hasn't seen anyone since doing a home test."

Another pause.

"Okay, best thing would be to send her straight to Berrivale Women's Health first for a dating scan and to check everything's alright with the pregnancy. They'll fax the report to us straight after, and then Dr. Roberts can see her later this afternoon with all the info in front of her."

Hope nodded, even though Natalie couldn't see. "Got it. Should I call Berrivale first?"

"No need. I'll ring ahead and tell them you're coming. You'll just need to be there by quarter past two to squeeze her in. They're flat out today."

"Thanks, Natalie. We appreciate it."

"No worries, love. Tell the young lady we'll take good care of her."

Hope ended the call and turned back to Ruby, who was still perched on the edge of the mattress, chewing her thumbnail.

"Well," Hope said gently. "They want us to pop over to Berrivale for an ultrasound before we see the doctor here. Just to check how far along you are and that everything's okay."

Ruby's eyes widened slightly. "Today?"

"Yes, now. I'll drive you. They've squeezed you in."

Ruby shrugged slightly, trying for nonchalance. "Alright, I guess."

But Hope didn't miss the way she smoothed her hand over her belly again, like she was both bracing herself and trying to offer comfort.

Fifteen minutes later, they were in the car. Ruby sat quietly in the passenger seat, arms folded, face turned to the passing hills. The road to Berrivale curved through singed bush and untouched paddocks. They were driving through a landscape of life and death.

The silence stretched for a while. Then Ruby spoke, her voice barely louder than the hum of the tyres.

"I keep thinking about what I'm giving up."

Hope glanced at her, then back to the road.

"Like what?"

"I don't know ... being eighteen. Doing stuff just for me. Travelling. Late nights out, long mornings sleeping in. Falling in love without baggage." She paused. "I feel like ... if I go through with this, I'll never be free again."

Hope was quiet for a moment before answering.

"It's a huge thing, Ruby. And it's okay to feel scared. This changes everything."

Ruby nodded, eyes still fixed on the road ahead.

Hope didn't want Ruby to feel pushed. "This isn't about what anyone else thinks you should do," she said quietly. "I just want you to know that you are cared for, and I want you to have all the information to make your own decision."

Ruby's voice was low. "It just means ... giving up so much."

Hope continued, her voice thoughtful. "A few nights ago, at the fire, there were people out there—firefighters, neighbours, even Joe—risking their lives to keep others safe. Running toward danger. That kind of sacrifice doesn't look heroic in the moment. It just looks like smoke and fear and exhaustion."

She glanced sideways.

"But those sacrifices ... they matter. They save lives."

Ruby's mouth tightened slightly as her defensive guard went up.

"You think this is the same?" Ruby challenged.

"I think it's different. But I also think choosing to give someone life is never a small thing." She paused. "You have options. And whatever you choose, I'll stand with you. But I guess I just want to ask … Is sacrificing your freedom too great a cost, if it means giving someone else a chance to live?"

Ruby didn't answer straight away. She looked out the window, one hand resting protectively across her belly. Her silence wasn't a refusal. It was the kind of quiet that meant she was really thinking.

Hope didn't press. Some seeds need room to settle before they begin to grow.

***

The waiting room at Berrivale Women's Health was calm and clean, with pale green walls and soft music playing overhead. Ruby sat stiffly beside Hope, her hoodie sleeves pulled down over her hands, her arms wrapped around her waist.

A nurse called her name, and Hope stood with her. Ruby hesitated.

"Do you want me to come in?" Hope asked gently.

Ruby gave the smallest nod.

The ultrasound room was softly lit, warm against the chill outside. The sonographer, a middle-aged woman with kind eyes, introduced herself as Leah and explained the process in a calm, professional tone.

Ruby lay back, lifting her jumper slightly while Leah applied a smooth layer of gel to her stomach. Ruby flinched. It was colder than expected, but she said nothing.

Then Leah pressed the probe to Ruby's lower belly and turned the screen.

It took a few seconds. Then a flickering form appeared. It was small but unmistakably shaped. A rhythmic pulsing filled the room.

"There," Leah said softly. "That's the heartbeat."

Ruby blinked. Her mouth parted slightly, but no words came out.

Leah continued, measuring and adjusting. "Everything looks healthy. You're just over twelve weeks, so you're moving into the second trimester. That's probably why the cramping's picking up. As you noted on your intake form, your body's adjusting."

Ruby nodded, eyes fixed on the screen. The flickering heartbeat continued, fast and determined.

"Do you want a photo?" Leah asked.

Ruby hesitated again, then nodded.

Hope reached for a tissue and gently handed it to Ruby, who hadn't noticed the tears slipping down her cheeks until now.

***

They drove in silence for a little while, the fading afternoon sun brushing the tops of the trees with gold.

Ruby held the black-and-white ultrasound image in her lap. She kept looking down at it, then back out the window.

Finally, she spoke.

"It looks like a real baby."

Hope didn't respond. She didn't need to.

CHAPTER 17

After the fire, Joe's clinic overflowed with the wounded and wild. There were koalas with scorched paws, echidnas dazed from smoke, and orphaned joeys curled in makeshift pouches. The place smelled of eucalyptus balm and warm milk. With Sarah only working part-time, and wildlife carers overwhelmed, Joe was running on fumes. He was sleep-deprived, overwhelmed, but too stubborn to slow down.

Pastor Tom had noticed. After dropping by one morning and seeing Joe cradling a singed wombat with one arm while bottle-feeding a joey with the other, he'd quietly spoken to Eve. Later that day, Eve phoned Joe with a suggestion.

"Nova?" he'd repeated.

"She trained as a nurse," Eve said. "It's a few years since she's worked in the job, but the skills are similar and she's steady. Gentle. Nova's ready to start giving back to others."

Joe remembered how Nova had calmly cared for Daisy while her leg was healing. The way she crouched quietly beside her and didn't say much, just offered reassurance and warmth.

He said yes.

The bell jingled sharply as Nova stepped into the clinic, wind tugging at her long brown hair. The waiting room smelled faintly of disinfectant. From the back, the low whine of a restless dog filtered through.

Joe appeared in the hallway, sleeves rolled to the elbows, and his usual quiet focus wrapped around him like armour.

"You're here," he said.

Nova gave a small shrug. "You said you needed help."

"I do," he said, without hesitation. "Come through."

She walked past the small reception desk, which was empty except for a thermos and Sarah's unfinished charting, the only signs of order in the chaos. The back room was full. Crates and carry baskets lined one wall. A young wombat dozed in a laundry basket beside a badly singed possum curled in a towel. The fridge hummed beneath the shelves, crowded with bottles of saline and medicated cream.

"It's like Noah's Ark in here," Nova murmured.

Joe smiled faintly. "Only slightly more chaotic than a flood. Sarah's off this morning, and most local wildlife carers are overloaded."

He handed her a clipboard and motioned to a stack of soft flannelette squares. "Can you start with fresh towels for the joeys and check their feeding logs to see if they're due? I've got a possum with a burned paw that's refusing to eat."

Nova nodded, slipping quickly into the rhythm of the place. It didn't take long for her movements to find purpose. She changed the towels, refilled a few water bottles, and offered a young wallaby joey its milk formula bottle, the animal's fragile body trembling with life.

But halfway through preparing another pouch bed, she froze. Nearby, curled tightly in a travel crate, lay a tiny sugar glider, its fur scorched along one side. It barely looked alive.

Nova crouched, reaching in gently. As her fingers brushed the fur, something in her expression cracked. A sob caught at her throat before she could swallow it down.

Joe looked up sharply from across the room. He came over quietly, crouching beside her.

"Hey," he said gently.

Nova shook her head, eyes wet. "I don't even know why I'm crying. It's just … it's so small and helpless. And it didn't deserve this."

Joe rested a hand lightly on her back. Not lingering. Just steady. "You've seen a lot of damage in life, Nova. Not just what you're seeing in here."

She closed her eyes. "It's stupid. I should be stronger than this."

"It's not stupid," Joe said. "And you're stronger than you know. You, Lily, and Daisy are safe because of your strength."

Nova nodded, not answering, but not pulling away. She took a shaky breath, and Joe stood, stepping back to give her space.

"I'll get you a glass of water," he said.

She didn't thank him with words, but the way she met his eyes for just a moment said more than enough.

When he returned, she was sitting on the stool by the door, gently feeding the tiny glider from a syringe.

The hum of the clinic filled the space between them again. But something had shifted.

Not romance. Not flirtation.

Just trust and safety. Fragile, hard-won, and rarely offered.

***

Hope carried the cake carefully, the tin still warm beneath the tea towel she'd wrapped it in. Lemon and poppyseed scents curled upward.

She'd found this recipe in Anna Butler's handwritten recipe book, after spending weeks looking through the recipes and baking a few to include in the café's cake fridge. Today though she had wanted to bake one just for

Joe. She wanted it to be a surprise. A thank you, perhaps. A small kindness returned.

The air was cooler than she expected as she walked up the road across the bridge and along the main street of Wombat Valley to the vet clinic. The sky was pale today, with hints of smoke on the breeze. For many, life had moved on from the bushfire scare last week, however, for others, life would never be the same again.

Hope reached the vet clinic front door and was about to knock when she noticed it was already slightly ajar. The little bell above it jingled only softly as she pushed it open.

Voices drifted from the back room. They sounded gentle, low, and close. She stepped inside quietly, not wanting to startle anyone. And then she paused.

Down the hallway she could see into the rear open clinic room. Joe was crouched beside Nova, who was visibly shaken. There was an animal Nova was holding, but all Hope could see was the closeness of the moment between them.

Nova's shoulders were tense, her eyes cast downward. Joe's voice was low, too soft to make out, but it carried that same gentle tone he'd used with Ruby, with sick animals, even once or twice with her. It sounded steady, kind and sure. He handed Nova a glass of water, with his hand brushing hers.

Hope froze, the cake still warm in her hands.

Something in her chest shifted. Not jealousy, not really. But something quieter. A sense of stepping in and being where she didn't belong.

She knew, better than most, how a woman looks when she's holding in more than she knows how to carry. She knew the tremble of hands, the look of grief still raw. And Joe, of course he would be kind. Of course, he would be gentle and caring. That's who he was.

But something in the softness between them, which was unspoken and unlabelled, felt suddenly like a closed door.

Hope stepped back quietly, her hands tightening slightly around the tea towel. She turned before the bell could jingle again and slipped outside. Her heart ached in a way she hadn't expected.

She didn't see Joe glance up a few seconds later, frown briefly at the empty doorway, and then stand to return quietly to the work at hand.

As Hope walked back to the café, the cake, still warm in her hands, felt like something she needed to protect, but no longer something meant to be shared.

***

Late afternoon light streamed through the café windows, catching flour in the air. Ruby wiped down tables after a quiet lunch shift, her movements were slower, and more thoughtful.

Hope had kept the day steady, with her head down, sleeves rolled, and heart quietly guarded.

She didn't want to think about this morning. About the cake still sitting in the pantry. About the way Joe had looked at Nova. What she'd seen or maybe imagined. Either way, it wasn't hers to hold.

The café bell gave a soft jingle.

Hope turned, heart giving a quiet jolt despite herself.

Joe stood in the doorway, framed by late light and the sounds of distant bird songs. Broad-chested and clean-shaven, he looked like he belonged more to the land than the room. He was strong, quiet, and solid. His shirt stretched slightly across his shoulders as he cradled a small canvas sling, held close with both arms.

The movement inside it was subtle, barely a twitch, but it caught Ruby's eye instantly.

Joe's gaze found Hope's, steady and unreadable.

"Thought you might be able to help someone."

Ruby dropped the cloth she'd been wiping the table with. "Is that a joey?"

He stepped forward, his gait relaxed but careful, like a man who knew how to handle those who were vulnerable. Gently, he folded back the edge of the sling to reveal a tiny wallaby. Its eyes were still closed, ears just beginning to unfurl. It was curled in a flannel pouch no longer than Joe's forearm, fragile and tucked in on itself.

The joey stirred, letting out a tiny sound.

"Lost his mum in the fire," Joe explained. "Too young to be weaned, only five or six months old, but a fighter. We're short on hands at the clinic and I thought … maybe Ruby would want to help bottle-feed him for a while. Just until we find a carer placement."

Ruby was already halfway across the room. "Oh, please. I'll be so careful."

Joe crouched as Ruby knelt beside him, gently cradling the pouch while he showed her how to put on the sling and support the little joey's body.

"He'll need feeding every four hours to start with. I've got the special formula and bottles here. One's ready to go, and inside are the instructions for the rest. Keep him warm, quiet, wrapped up like this. He'll mostly sleep between feeds."

Ruby's expression softened with something close to awe. "He's perfect."

Hope gave a faint smile as Ruby fed the joey with surprising ease, her small hands instinctively gentle. She watched her rock the bundle like it was the most natural thing in the world.

Hope softened. "You've got a good touch," she said quietly.

Joe stood and brushed his hands on his jeans.

"He's in good hands, Ruby. And you've got Hope here if you need anything."

There was a beat of silence. Hope didn't look up. She nodded slightly but kept her focus on the counter, picking up a dish towel and folding it without purpose.

Joe moved closer, lowering his voice.

"I was going to drop by yesterday. Thought maybe we could—"

He paused, noticing how her gaze stayed down, and her posture tightened.

"Everything alright?"

Hope nodded, too quickly. "Fine. Just busy. I've got Rowena starting tomorrow, so I'm getting things ready."

Joe's kind eyes watched her. Reading more than she wanted him to.

"Hope, if something's bothering you …"

"I'm glad you brought him," she said softly, cutting him off, eyes still on the towel. "Ruby's needed something to distract her."

A pause.

Joe's voice dropped further. "Alright then."

He didn't press. Just gave a small nod, crouched again to say something kind to Ruby, who was now crooning softly to the bundle in her arms, and then quietly made his way to the door.

Hope turned back to the counter, wiping down an already clean surface, her throat tight.

When she finally glanced toward the entrance again, he was gone.

Outside, the wind stirred through the trees.

Inside, Hope let her hand rest on the counter and closed her eyes.

She wasn't sure what she'd been guarding against more, disappointment or possibility.

CHAPTER 18

The cottage sat at the far edge of Edith and Rob's property, tucked between a paddock of knee-high grass and a windbreak of slender gums. Weathered white paint flaked from the boards, and the verandah sloped slightly, but the roof was good, and the walls were sound. It looked like a place that had been waiting patiently to matter again.

Rowena stood at the front steps, fingers clenched around the worn strap of her overnight bag. She'd packed it in minutes, with clothes, keepsakes, and whatever she could grab before the fire took the rest. Behind her, Hope carried a box of pantry staples. Eve followed with fresh linen, blankets, and a bag of groceries.

Hope pushed the door open. A breath of pine smoke and old wood drifted out. Edith had lit the hearth that morning. The cottage exhaled warmth.

Rowena didn't move.

Hope set the box on the kitchen bench and turned. "You alright?"

Rowena gave a short nod, her eyes fixed on the floorboards just inside the door.

Eve came up beside her, voice gentle. "There's no rush. It's just a space. Nothing permanent."

Rowena let out a breath and stepped over the threshold.

Inside, the cottage was spare but clean. A faded armchair sat by the wood stove, a table and two mismatched chairs in the corner. The bed was made with a crocheted blanket, its colours sun-faded but still warm.

Rowena crossed to the window. Cows grazed in the paddock beyond, and a windmill creaked slowly in the breeze.

"It's strange," she murmured. "To look out a window and not see the garden. No rows of greens. No vegetables."

Eve smiled gently. "One day, you will again."

Rowena shook her head, folding her arms across her chest. "I don't know. After the fire … it wasn't just the house. It was everything. Every fence post we dug, every seed we planted. It's all gone. Just ash and broken glass."

Hope moved closer but didn't reach for her.

She knew that feeling too well. The aching exhaustion of starting over. How loss seeps into your skin, into your bones. How even something hopeful, like fresh sheets or a warm room, can feel like too much to touch at first. And how hard it is to let yourself believe that anything can still be yours.

Rowena's voice dropped. "I didn't realise how loud it would be."

Hope frowned. "What?"

She looked over. "The silence. After it's all gone."

The room held stillness like breath.

Then Eve spoke, quiet but sure. "We don't always get to keep the lives we built. But sometimes, by grace, we get a second chance to build something different."

Tears filled Rowena's eyes. She didn't blink them away.

"My husband died ten years ago," she said suddenly. "Heart failure. He was forty-two. We started the market garden together. After he died, I kept it going, for the kids, and for myself. Then they'd grown and left. But now …" Her voice faltered.

Hope stepped beside her. "And now you're still here."

Rowena nodded, tears slipping down her cheeks. "Yes. I'm still here."

The fire popped in the hearth behind them. A magpie warbled from the fence post outside.

Hope turned back to the bench and unpacked a jar of homemade preserves, setting it gently beside the bread and eggs. "You've got food, fresh sheets, and a warm fire. It's not much, but it's a start."

Rowena gave a watery smile. "That's more than enough."

She moved to the bedroom door, paused, then looked back.

"Thank you. Both of you."

Eve stepped forward, resting a hand over hers. "You're not alone. Wombat Valley takes care of its own. Especially the ones who think they have nothing left."

Rowena nodded again. Her shoulders still sagged, but her hands were open now. Not clenched.

Hope watched her disappear into the bedroom.

She didn't say it aloud, but she knew the truth of it: rebuilding didn't come in grand gestures. It came in warm bread. In not flinching when someone touched your hand. In walking into a room and letting yourself believe, maybe, you could belong again.

A beginning.

***

Mid-morning, Hope unlocked the café back door and flicked on the lights one by one as she moved through the kitchen. She filled the kettle, checked the sourdough starter, and laid out her prep list.

Hope had told herself Rowena's first shift would be simple, just some prep work, maybe roast a tray of vegetables for the winter salad. Nothing too heavy.

She was halfway through peeling a bucket of carrots when the back door creaked and boots shuffled softly across the tiles.

Rowena stepped in, apron already tied around her waist. "I hope you don't mind me coming in early. I unpacked my bag in minutes and don't have anything else to focus on right now. Here are some parsnips that Edith left for us in the kitchen."

Hope offered a quiet smile and nodded toward the chopping board. "That's your spot, then."

Rowena moved easily around the kitchen, her hands finding knives, trays, and herbs with a seasoned knowledge of where things should be. She didn't ask permission for every step, but she didn't assume anything, either. It was a kind of dance. Hope led at first, then let Rowena fall into step beside her.

They worked mostly in silence. Carrots, pumpkin, beetroot, and parsnip were peeled, tossed in oil and cumin, and laid on baking trays. The scent of thyme and garlic began to rise, deep and comforting.

Behind them, Ruby wandered in, still in pyjamas, the joey curled in a sling against her chest, ears twitching. Her hands moved instinctively to calm him, as she padded to the back counter and began setting out cutlery.

Rowena glanced over. "He looks content in that pouch."

Ruby smiled. "He twitches sometimes in his sleep.

I wonder if he's remembering the fire.

When he does, I hum."

She began a soft melody. The joey stilled, his breathing slow and rhythmic.

"That baby's going to be lucky," Rowena said quietly, "if you choose to keep it."

Ruby didn't know which baby she meant, so she just hummed a little louder.

Hope caught Rowena's eye, then returned to the soup simmering on the stove. Rowena had made a few quiet adjustments to the pumpkin and carrot base. She'd added cumin, garlic, and a pinch of smoked paprika. The air smelled of warm spices.

Rowena dipped a spoon in and offered it across. "What do you think?"

Hope tasted it slowly. Let it sit. "Smokey Carrot and Pumpkin," she said. "That's going on the board."

They smiled at each other, it was tentative, but a connection.

***

As lunchtime rolled in, Rowena stepped out from behind the counter, a tray of still-warm savoury muffins in hand, her hair pinned up, apron dusted with flour. She greeted a local couple with an easy warmth and offered them a sample.

Hope stood in the kitchen doorway, arms folded. Watching.

It felt strange to share the rhythm of this place, but not wrong.

She stepped back and saw Ruby curled on her mattress in the store-room, the joey tucked into the crook of her arm, both fast asleep. Hope crossed the room quietly and pulled a nearby blanket over them.

The late-night feeds were taking their toll. So was everything else.

When she turned back, Rowena was watching from the doorway.

"Looks like we've found ourselves a little family," she said gently.

Hope didn't answer right away. Her heart hadn't yet decided how to feel about that.

But as she glanced around the kitchen, with the stock bubbling, the muffins cooling, and the air rich with the scent of cumin and thyme. Hope felt something ease. Not joy, not certainty. Just … quiet.

Maybe this was what rebuilding safely looked like. No grand gestures.

Just hands moving side by side. A soup left to simmer. A joey dreaming. A girl sleeping safely under a warm blanket.

Hope reached for a second spoon and passed it to Rowena.

It wasn't just food.

It was healing work, for both of them.

CHAPTER 19

Craig arrived at the vet clinic with Diesel, his old blue heeler limping stiffly beside him. The cold leading into winter was setting into the valley early this year, and Diesel's joints were feeling it. Inside, the familiar scent of antiseptic and hay lingered, and Joe looked up from the treatment bench with a grin that came easy between old friends.

"Could've just sent him in with a note," Joe said, bending to greet the dog. Diesel wagged his tail like they were all part of the same pack.

"Thought he'd get special treatment if I came in person," Craig replied, scratching behind his dog's ear.

They eased into conversation the way men do, when they've weathered life seasons and the slow turning of years. While Joe measured out anti-inflammatory tablets, Craig mentioned that his boys, Ben and Nate, were due back this weekend from the city for the school holidays.

"Might be good to get them out of town for a bit," Craig said, voice thoughtful. "Shake the smoke off. Maybe head up the riverbend for a night."

Joe looked up. "Haven't camped there in years."

"Still the same old wombat holes and flat ground. Just quiet. And the water's clear."

Joe nodded slowly, the idea beginning to spark. "You reckon Hope and Ruby might want in? Nova and Lily too? Might do them good."

Later that afternoon, Joe stopped by the café. The scent of cinnamon and baked scones met him at the door. Hope looked up from wiping a bench, her brow furrowing as he explained.

"I don't have any good memories of 'sleeping on the ground'." Hope said. She actually wasn't sure if she wanted front-row seats to the kind of campfire honesty that tended to rise with smoke.

But Ruby's eyes lit up, and Rowena sensing something deeper in the invitation, offered to mind the café without hesitation. She mentioned that Edith had told her she was free this weekend if they needed an extra pair of hands. It would feel ungracious to say no now, so Hope accepted Joe's offer to join them. He said he'd come and pick them up.

While standing in the café, Joe also rang Nova, who accepted the invitation with surprising readiness. "Lily needs space to run," she said. "And so do I." Joe shared Nova's response with the other women. Hope felt strangely reassured, and wondered if she might have placed more significance on the interaction she had seen in the vet clinic than was merited.

***

On Friday afternoon, they packed swags and folding chairs, marshmallows, enamel mugs, and a thermos of Hope's spiced chai. They drove in convoy, with the two utes and Nova's hatchback bumping slowly along the track, then slowed as they approached a riverbend.

And there it was: a patch of remembered peace. Tall gums leaning over the river. Flat grassy banks, soft underfoot. The water coming down from the nearby Southern Highlands ran clear and quiet, carrying stories of rain and time from higher ground. A space that hadn't burned.

***

Later that evening, the fire crackled and snapped, casting a soft light on the circle of folding chairs and log seats drawn close around it. A chorus of frogs called from the riverbank, and the sky above was a clear velvet blanket, pinpricked with stars. Somewhere upstream, an owl hooted, then fell silent.

Ben and Nate had just finished roasting marshmallows, triumphant with their golden-brown perfection. Lily, face sticky with sugar and soot, curled up against Nova, quietly humming a tune only she seemed to remember.

Craig poured billy tea into mismatched enamel mugs, his movements calm, capable and unhurried. His sons teased him affectionately as he handed one to Nova.

"Careful," he warned gently, "it's hotter than it looks."

Nova reached to take it, and for the briefest second their hands touched. She flinched, just enough that most would miss it, but not Craig. He didn't react, just settled back onto his log with his own mug and watched the flames.

Across the fire, Joe leaned back in his chair, one boot propped on a nearby log. He looked relaxed, more so than Hope had seen him in weeks. He was telling a story about when he and Craig had camped here years ago, and a wombat had eaten their breakfast cereal.

"Craig swore it must have been a dingo," Joe said with a grin. "Woke up ready to wrestle it."

Craig raised his mug. "Well … he had criminal intent."

The group laughed. Even Nova smiled.

Hope sat next to Ruby, who was feeding small pieces of damper to the joey now bundled up in a sling across her front. The joey's ears twitched at the sounds of laughter, his little face peeking out like a wise, sleepy elder.

Hope watched the firelight flicker across Joe's face, the ease of his friendship with Craig, the way he leaned in to listen when others spoke. She remembered the cake in her pantry, and the ache that had bloomed when she saw him with Nova. But now, she saw something else. Not the risk of being hurt. Just the constancy of a man who showed up.

Across the circle, Nova was pulling Lily's beanie back down over her ears. Craig reached into the firelight and offered her a marshmallow on a stick.

She hesitated again. Then, slowly, took it.

"I haven't had one of these since Lily's dad …" she murmured, so softly Hope barely caught it. "We used to camp before … things changed."

Craig didn't pry. He just said, "It's alright to start new memories. *Even* around old ghosts."

Nova looked at him squarely for the first time that night. There was no pity in his eyes. Just quiet recognition. She gave the smallest nod and turned back to the fire.

Ruby shifted closer to Hope and whispered, "Craig and his sons are nice, aren't they?"

Hope glanced at Nova, then Craig, then Joe, who had just handed Nate his jacket when the boy pretended not to be cold.

"They are," she said softly. "It's a different kind of strength."

Ruby rested her head on Hope's shoulder. The gesture was unexpected but oddly comforting. "Do you think we'll ever be relaxed like that? Just kicking back and enjoying what life has to offer?"

Hope watched the flames, the flicker of them reflected in Ruby's tired eyes. "I think we're already on our way."

The fire popped as a log split, sparks rising into the sky. For a long while, no one said anything. They just watched the stars and listened to the sound of water, in the hush that only comes in places untouched by time.

Then, a wombat ambled into the edge of the firelight without warning. It paused, slowly turned, and lumbered on. Lily stirred in Nova's lap, half-awake. "We really saw a wombat," she murmured sleepily, then as the creature moved away into the darkness, she drifted off to sleep again in her mother's arms.

Hope looked across the fire. Joe's gaze met hers—and this time, she didn't look away.

She wondered, if the friendship, that had been interrupted in her mind, could begin again.

***

After Nova said goodnight and took Lily off to their tent, Ruby and Hope walked down to the edge of the river to wash up the mugs. Frogs croaked nearby.

Ruby tilted her head back, eyes tracing the scatter of stars overhead. "It's the first time in weeks I feel like I can actually breathe."

Hope smiled, pulling her jacket tighter. "You're not the only one."

A quiet pause passed between them.

Ruby glanced over. "Do you think people can really have more than one beginning?"

Hope looked up again thoughtfully. "I think that beginnings come in all kinds of ways. Some are gentle. Some feel like survival. Some we never asked for." She paused, then added, "But even the hard ones … sometimes they open a door we couldn't see before."

Ruby reflected on this as they finished shaking the water off the mugs. The clinking of enamel was soft in the dark.

Back at the campfire, Joe offered to look after Ember tonight. "It will give you a chance to sleep all night through," he offered. "It also means that Hope won't be woken as you shuffle about getting the bottle ready for him."

Ruby smiled tiredly and nodded, gratefully handing him over. The fire crackled softly as she said goodnight, stepping away into the darkness.

As Joe adjusted the sling around his chest, Hope sat back down near the warmth.

The fire had burned low, embers glowing in ash, casting a soft orange light across the grass. Only the sounds of crickets and frogs could now be heard, and the occasional pop of sap that echoed into the dark like a distant sparkler.

On the other side of the clearing, Craig's voice rose in mock frustration as he wrestled with tent poles and his two sons, who sounded more amused than helpful.

Hope sat on the same log she'd occupied earlier, staring into the fire like it might answer questions she hadn't quite dared ask.

The space between them was easy but charged, like standing on the edge of a conversation neither was sure how to begin.

He nudged the log with his boot. "You still awake, or just trying to stay up so you'll sleep through breakfast duty in the morning?"

Hope smiled faintly. "It's tempting."

There was a pause. Joe leaned forward, resting his arms on his knees, looking into the embers.

"I wasn't sure you'd come," he said softly.

Hope hesitated. "Neither was I."

Another pause. Not tense. Just cautious.

Joe glanced at her. "You seemed a little … distant a few days ago when I brought the joey to Ruby."

Hope nodded slowly, not denying it.

She weighed up whether to be honest for a moment. Then admitted, "I saw a moment with you and Nova."

Joe's brow furrowed, and Hope continued to explain. "I stopped in at the clinic the other day to give you something and saw what looked like a tender moment between you both," she said, voice low. "And I guess … I just wanted to step back."

Joe spoke in gentle confusion. "Nova? She's been through something awful. Whatever it looked like, that wasn't what you think."

"I know that" Hope said quickly. "At least, I do now. Because of my past, I've got a habit of running first and explaining later." Hope sighed deeply. "I'm starting to recognise some habits in myself that I need to take responsibility for, and change."

He breathed out deeply. After a moment, Joe spoke. "I'm not asking for anything, Hope. Not now. But I'm not going anywhere either."

Hope looked down into her cup, fingers tightening around it. "That's the hard part, Joe. For me. Learning to trust again. Knowing that people are who they say they are."

They sat in silence for a few moments, just the crackle of the fire and the rustle of breeze through gum leaves.

Then Joe spoke, quieter still. "You don't have to figure it all out tonight. But if there's ever a day you want to talk more about what trust looks like…"

Hope didn't answer.

But she looked up into his eyes, reflecting flickering flames of warmth, and smiled.

Tonight, that was enough.

CHAPTER 20

*N*ova, in leggings and a loose jumper, had just finished dinner with Lily while dusk settled in. As the dishwasher was being stacked, Lily asked if she could watch a favourite DVD. Nova agreed as long as she promised to brush her teeth and head to bed as soon as it was over.

The crunch of tyres on gravel near the granny flat made Nova freeze. Plate still in hand, Nova moved quietly to the front window and peered through the curtain.

By the verandah light, she saw Evan's four-wheel drive roll to a stop inside the gate.

Her chest tightened.

He didn't get out right away. Evan just sat there, with the engine ticking. Then the door creaked open. He walked down the path and stepped onto the porch like a shadow come to life.

Nova didn't want Lily to hear the conversation, so closed the door to the living area quietly. She opened front door, but stood behind the screen door and didn't step out.

"Evan," she said cautiously, her hand gripping the edge of the doorframe.

"Been trying to reach you." His voice was cool but clipped. "We need to talk."

Lily's giggle floated out from the living room. Nova shifted, placing herself more squarely in the doorway.

"Evan, you shouldn't be here."

"You said this was a break, not a separation. I gave you space. Now it's time to come home." His voice was cold.

Nova held her ground. "I'm not ready."

His jaw tightened. "You're making things complicated."

She shook her head, heart pounding. "You made things complicated, Evan. When you grabbed my arm. When you kicked Daisy so hard you injured her. When Lily cried and you didn't stop shaking me."

Having Nova bravely face him with truths, cracked his calm.

He stepped closer to the screen door, voice low and dangerous. "Don't push me, Nova. You think you can just run here to your church friends, and they'll fix everything?"

A tremble started in her legs, climbing like a wave. She clenched her jaw, swallowing it down.

"You need to leave." Her voice was low.

"Or what? You'll call the cops? Don't think you're safe here from me, Nova. I can come and get you anytime I want."

She didn't answer. Just shut the main door firmly and locked it.

Nova then grabbed her phone and rang Eve.

A minute later, she looked into the living room, Lily had paused the DVD and was staring at her from the couch, clutching her stuffed rabbit. Nova knelt and gathered her up.

"Where are we going?" Lily whispered.

"To visit Eve and Pastor Tom."

Within moments, Nova was standing on their back porch and Eve opened the door.

"Oh love," Eve said, pulling her in. "Come in. You're safe here."

***

Later that evening, Nova sat on the couch in Pastor Tom and Eve's living room. Lily had been tucked up in a spare bedroom a while ago and was now sleeping, wrapped in a plush soft blanket, tightly gripping her special rabbit toy.

A pot of tea with steam drifting upwards was sitting in the middle of the coffee table. Tom stood near the window, his arms folded. Eve was sitting beside Nova, calm and attentive, watching police officer Dave who had just arrived and taken a seat across from them.

Nova's hands were wrapped tightly around a mug of chamomile tea, but she hadn't touched it. Her fingers trembled every so often, betraying the effort she was making to hold herself together.

Officer Dave pulled his chair over in front of the couch. He was in his late forties, clean-shaven, with watchful eyes and a kind mouth. Nova had seen him around in town and sometimes dropping off his girls before school.

"Nova, I just need you to talk me through what happened. As best you can remember."

She hesitated, then gave a slow, shallow nod.

"I was finishing the dishes. I heard his car. He just appeared. Said it was time to come home. I told him no, and then he …" She swallowed. "He threatened to come in and get me. He said we weren't safe here."

Dave nodded once. "Did he try to come in the house?"

"No. But he didn't need to." She let out a shaky breath. "I've seen that look before. And I've seen what comes after it."

He didn't write anything down yet just looked at her. "Do you feel safe returning home, here behind Tom and Eve's place, tonight?"

"I don't know," she admitted, her voice barely above a whisper. "I hate that I even have to think like that. That I can't protect my own daughter."

"You're not weak," Eve said gently, reaching over to squeeze her hand. "You're responding to a threat. That's wisdom, not failure."

Dave stood and reached for the small folder tucked under his arm. "Nova, you have options. I can help you apply for an interim Apprehended Domestic Violence Order tonight. It'll mean Evan legally can't approach you, your home, or Lily's school, without risk of immediate arrest."

Nova glanced toward the bedroom where Lily slept.

"Will that just make him angrier?" Her voice cracked, the fear breaking through despite everything she was trying to hold in.

"Yes," Dave said simply. "Possibly. But if you continue to stay on a property living with or near others, it should make you safer. The ADVO gives us grounds to act if he steps out of line again."

Pastor Tom shifted from his place at the window. "You're not alone in this. We welcomed you and Lily to stay here because we want to help to protect and support you."

There was silence.

Nova nodded slowly. "Okay," she said, her voice catching. "I want to do it."

Eve leaned over, her voice warm and resolute. "You are choosing courage, Nova. And Lily will grow up knowing what that looks like."

Nova blinked, trying to steady herself. "I just want her to feel safe."

"She will," Dave said, already unfolding the paperwork with quiet steadiness.

"And with help and support, so will you."

***

The next morning, a mellow sun warmed the café yard as Hope stepped out to greet Craig, who'd come over to give her advice about some small building alterations.

Craig's ute pulled up in a soft cloud of dust. He stepped out and reached down to pat Asha, who bounded over to greet him.

"You said to swing by if I had time to look at that shower idea."

She smiled and leaned on her broom. "Still keen if you are available. Ruby's been using my shower, but it'd be good for her to have her own space."

Craig nodded, brow furrowed. "Teenagers need their own space. Especially ones learning to feel safe again."

They moved around the back toward the storeroom. Inside, Craig walked across the back wall, tapping timber panels thoughtfully.

"You could fit a basic wet room here, no worries. Hook it into the water line that runs behind the café's amenities. I've got a mate with some spare fittings; he owes me a favour."

"And a dog door?" Hope asked, smiling faintly. "Could we install one here in the external storeroom door?"

"That's the easy bit." He grinned. "You want Asha to have her own key, do you?"

"More like she's getting too big to sleep in Ruby's arms all night," Hope said. "But she still needs to go out, and it wakes Ruby to do this and then let her back in."

As Craig tapped and measured the space, Hope asked him a deeper question that she hadn't wanted to raise in front of his boys over the weekend.

"How's Therese going?"

Craig stopped, leaned back on his knees and sighed.

"Therese says she can't do the farm life anymore. It's not what she signed up for." He didn't sound bitter, just steady, with the kind of honest acceptance that comes from seeing what's ahead. "I reckon, with her renting the unit in the city to have a break at the beginning of the year, I knew it was coming. But it still stings, you know."

Hope listened and felt a quiet solidarity in Craig's words. After a few beats, she replied, "It's hard to find a compromise when both people aren't coming to the table."

Realising Craig might misread her meaning, she added, "I mean, it's hard to keep sharing a life with someone who doesn't want to build one with you."

Craig nodded. They let the silence settle, companionable and reflective, as birds called out in the gumtrees overhead.

Outside again, a breeze lifted a strand of Hope's hair. Craig caught sight of Ruby sitting under the mulberry tree, feeding the joey.

"You're doing a good job with her," he said quietly, and sincerely.

Hope smiled. "She's helping me see outside myself. And with the joey, she's reminding us both what nurture looks like."

Craig's gaze drifted toward the café. "You've built something special here. Don't think you'll be slowing down anytime soon."

Hope looked at him. He was solid, steady, and offering kindness without expectation.

"Thanks, Craig. If the storeroom modifications come in within budget, I'm keen to go ahead."

"I'll call you," he said, tipping his head in parting.

As he walked back toward his ute, Hope stood still for a moment, watching him go.

And she found herself wondering why some men, even after life had knocked them down, didn't feel the need to knock others down with them.

CHAPTER 21

*H*ope pressed her palms into the dough, watching it stretch beneath her fingers. The rhythm soothed her. It was something familiar. Practical. There was comfort in knowing that with the right ingredients, time and care, flour would always become bread.

The back door creaked open, and Nova slipped in with the quiet ease of someone who no longer needed permission to belong. Asha padded in behind her and flopped down near Ruby, who reached down absently to stroke her ears.

"You're up early," Hope said.

Nova smiled, shrugging. "Eve offered to look after Lily this morning so I could head out here to have a coffee." She looked longingly at the machine. "Instant coffee certainly doesn't hold a candle to your barista made flat white."

Hope smiled and began to make Nova one while she went and sought out Ruby's joey to see how he was growing.

"He's begun hopping around the yard this week." Ruby announced like a proud Mum.

Nova recognised the tone and smiled. As she turned to offer payment to Hope, who waved her away, Nova spoke. "Tom said he's sharing something at the nine o'clock service, for people who are still finding their way to faith. I thought I'd be brave and go along."

Hope glanced up, as she returned to work on the dough. "You're actually thinking of going to church?"

"Mm-hmm." Nova took a sip of her cup.

Hope's hands didn't stop moving. The dough was nearly there—smooth and soft, like skin. She didn't speak, but she was listening.

"I know it's not everyone's thing," Nova said, resting on a stool behind the counter. "But spending time in the company of Tom and Eve has helped me to settle. To understand what's important, and to let things some things go."

Ruby looked up from her breakfast. "Could I come?"

Hope turned to her, surprised.

Ruby shrugged, cheeks slightly pink. "I just wanna see what it's like. Not promising I'll sing hymns or anything."

Nova grinned. "You won't have to. I imagine most people just stand there humming, anyway."

"I don't know," Hope said softly. "It's been a long time since I have been inside a church. I wouldn't even know what to do anymore."

"I don't think you have to do anything," Nova replied gently. "Just come and sit with us. That's all."

Hope didn't answer straight away.

She wiped her hands on a tea towel. Her pulse fluttered, unexpectedly. She wasn't sure why.

Hope looked out the back window. The first light of morning touched the tops of the gums behind the cottage, golden and tentative.

A whisper stirred in her. Not certainty.

But perhaps … willingness.

***

Hope sat straight-backed, shoulders tight despite herself. The pew was hard, just like she remembered. The air smelled faintly of varnish and furniture polish. It seemed too clean. She hadn't set foot in a church in years. Not since it stopped feeling like a place where she was welcome.

Nova sat beside her, calm and anchored. Ruby on Hope's other side leaned forward slightly, curious.

Tom opened his Bible slowly and looked out over the room. His voice, when it came, was quiet. Not theatrical. Not striving. Not performing for an audience.

"Some of you are carrying things you don't know how to put down. Hurt you didn't ask for. Shame that was never yours to carry. And possibly, choices in life that have caused pain to yourself or others."

Hope's breath caught in her throat. She looked down, blinking quickly. Tom went on.

"There's a story in Luke's gospel, a story most of us know. The prodigal son. We think it's a story about running away and coming back. But it's not just about the son. It's about the Father, too. A Father who ran as soon as he saw his child returning. Who didn't wait for the right words. Who didn't need the perfect apology."

He paused. His voice dropped lower.

"But here's the part we can't skip over. The son *did* turn around. That's what repentance means. It's not just about walking away from the wrong path, it begins with a moment of truth. A recognition that something isn't right in our life. That moves us to turn around with a heart that is sorry toward the One who is good, who is full of grace and truth, and who meets us with the power to heal and make us whole.

Turning is not about shame. It's not about self-hatred. But instead about having a change of heart, and making a choice to come home, to the loving Father who has been waiting for us all along."

He let that hang for a moment.

"When the son came to his senses, he got up and went home. And even when he was still far off, the Father saw and ran to welcome him."

Hope's throat tightened. She hadn't expected this. Not the ache. Not the yearning. Not the sharp memory of what it was like to feel unworthy in a place meant for mercy.

She glanced toward the front and caught sight of Joe.

He was sitting quietly, eyes lowered, hands loosely folded in his lap. He wasn't trying to be seen. There was something about the way he listened, as if the words were sinking deep, taking root, that made Hope's chest ache.

Tom's voice was tender now.

"You don't need to clean yourself off before you come to God. But you do have to come. And turning … saying yes to Him … that's what opens the door. That's what brings you home to be forgiven and welcomed into His family."

He closed his Bible gently.

"No matter how far you've gone, no matter what shape you're in … you are not too far away to turn around. You are never beyond the reach of the Father's love."

Hope let her eyes close for a moment. Just long enough to breathe.

She hadn't planned to feel anything. But something in her had begun to stir.

Not everything could be healed in a day.

But, she wondered, could this be the start of something new?

**

The church lawn was dappled with shade from the overhead trees. Hope weaved through small clusters of people chatting and watched children laughing and chasing one another outside the hall. She'd bypassed the folding table of tea, coffee, and biscuits without stopping, and was just about to call Ruby so they could head back to the café, when she spotted Joe walking down the steps with his guitar slung over one shoulder.

He saw her before she could look away and offered that same steady smile, warm and unassuming, with nothing behind it but presence.

"Hey," he said as he reached her. "I'm glad you came."

Hope smiled, though it felt tentative. "Still not sure if it was courage or foolishness."

He glanced over at Ruby, who was now deep in conversation with Eve and Nova over the biscuit tin, then turned back to Hope. "How was it for you? Really?"

She took a slow breath. "Strange. Hard. Good, I think … in a way I wasn't expecting." A pause. "Tom's message, it didn't feel like pressure. It felt like a door cracking open."

Joe nodded. "That's him. He doesn't try to impress anyone. Just opens the Word and lets it speak."

Hope studied him for a moment. "You sing like someone who believes it."

Joe's expression softened.

Hope held his gaze, trying to see what shaped him.

She searched for the right words. "The church I used to attend had a polished music team. Very talented. But sometimes it felt more like a performance ... than worship."

Joe nodded, understanding. "That's why I asked Tom if I could stand to the side when I sing. I don't ever want it to be about me."

Hope absorbed this, hearing not just what he said but who he was.

She looked down for a moment, then said quietly, "I wasn't sure I'd ever sit in a church again without the panic kicking in. Too many hard memories. Being judged instead of helped. Feeling alone. Watching people support the person who was hurting me."

Joe was silent for a moment, nodding slowly, the weight of her words settling between them.

"There's no timeline for healing," he said gently. "Just courage ... space ... and grace to begin again."

***

Joe's words echoed in Hope's mind in the car on the way back to the café.

Ruby broke the silence. "What was Pastor Tom saying about grace?"

Hope revisited the sermon in her mind, sorting through its pieces. "I think he was saying it's something God offers freely to anyone willing to receive it."

Ruby frowned thoughtfully. "Is grace about acceptance, or forgiveness?"

"Both ... I think." Hope glanced at her. "Maybe even love, offered before you've earned it. That's probably a good question to ask Eve, or Tom."

As the trees blurred past the window, Hope felt something stir, something she hadn't dared feel in a long time. Not certainty. But a curiosity and openness to start hearing again.

She thought of her grandmother's old Bible on the bedside table, only opened tentatively a couple of times. Maybe it was time to read it. Not to have all the answers. But to see what God wanted to say to her.

Perhaps being a wise mother figure didn't mean always knowing the answers but instead being willing to seek the truth.

CHAPTER 22

Ruby lay still in the half-light; eyes fixed on the landscape being revealed with the dawn. Beside her, Asha's soft breathing rose and fell, as she curled up and then stretched to readjust herself on the old, knitted blanket. Ember, the joey, was asleep in his pouch, which was bulging much more heavily as he was growing quickly.

Her hand rested on her belly. Not flat anymore. Not quite.

"I don't know if I can do this," she whispered into the quiet.

But the quiet wasn't empty. It held the weight of another memory, a clinic room, with the nurse's soft voice, and her mother's furious silence in the car afterward.

You're lucky, her mother had said. Don't mess up like this again.

Ruby hadn't cried. Not until much later. And even then, she hadn't known if she had done the right thing.

Outside, a currawong called through the trees. The day was moving forward. Even if she still felt stuck.

This time, no one had forced her. Not yet. And maybe … she wanted help. From someone who didn't just see the problem but saw her.

***

Ruby had been up and showered in her new ensuite that Craig had recently finished building, long before Hope appeared at the café's kitchen back door.

When she walked in and glanced around the café at the reset tables and freshly filled water jugs, she arched her brows and looked at Ruby.

"Is this your way of hinting that you deserve a pay rise?"

Ruby shook her head. "I was actually wondering if you and Row are able to cope without me, if I could have the day off?"

Hope looked concerned. "Are you okay?"

"Not really. I just need some space to think. A walk might help more than work today."

Hope slowly nodded, realising that today's outcome might be significant.

"Sure," she said. "We'll be able to cover the midday shift and even tonight if you'd like to take the whole day off. It sounds like important time for you to weigh some things up."

Ruby felt a lump forming in her throat, but managed to squeeze out, "thanks."

***

A while later, Ruby and Asha wandered along the main street and saw Eve kneeling next to the rose garden bed alongside the rectory. They slowly walked down to join her.

Eve noticed them and smiled. "Are you and Asha wagging off work today?"

The corner of Ruby's mouth turned up in response to her warm joking, but Eve noticed this didn't reach her troubled eyes.

"Do you have things on your mind today?" Eve gently asked, sensing the turbulence beneath the surface.

"I want to decide today whether to keep the baby. It's just hard to know what the right thing is."

Eve didn't jump in with an answer but just patted the grassy spot next to her encouraging Ruby to take a seat. Asha had already jumped at the invitation, lying down and rolling around on the grass nearby.

Ruby thought Eve would speak, but instead, she calmly kept pruning the rose bush in front of her.

"It might sound strange," Eve said a few minutes later, "but there is actually a lot of wisdom to learn from a rose bush."

Ruby couldn't think of any connection between roses and what she was thinking about.

Eve continued, "Rose bushes tell us a story about their life, what has worked, and what hasn't." She pointed to sections of the bush that had browned and died off, and other areas that were shooting growth even out of season. "Learn from the mistakes you have made before, and change to make good decisions going forward."

Ruby was listening carefully and thinking about her choice made last time.

Eve continued, "It's also helpful to know that the most beautiful flowers can grow from the harshest and ugliest stems. Ruby, you've had a hard upbringing. But that doesn't mean this will be the same life your baby will be born into. You have so many people around you now that care, and who want to help and support you."

Tears welled in Ruby's eyes as memories of her past washed over her: the ache of not feeling loved, and of never knowing if she was wanted.

Eve, sensing the battle inside her, wrapped Ruby's shoulders in a hug. Ruby stayed there. Feeling loved, feeling seen.

When Eve let go, Ruby felt something loosen inside, as if old chains of fear were beginning to slip away. Maybe she wasn't destined to live the life her mother had lived. She might be able to choose a new path for herself.

Ruby turned to where Asha lay in the sun. She stretched out beside her, the autumn warmth seeping into her back. For the first time in a long while, she closed her eyes. Not to block the world out, but to rest in it.

Eve turned to look at them both, silently praying that God would help Ruby to know that whatever her decision was about the baby, He loved them both deeply.

***

Ruby and Asha had noticed Daisy lurking in the garden as they said good-bye to Eve, tail twitching like she'd been waiting. Asha had rushed forward to see her canine companion and the two dogs greeted each other by sniffing scents before running off together to find lizards to terrify on the nearby riverbank. Ruby watched the dogs playing, but her thoughts didn't stray far. She still felt the weight of the question sitting in her heart.

Ruby was just about to call Asha back when she noticed Nova sitting on the verandah with a cup of tea, reading a book.

Wondering if there might be more wisdom to gather today, Ruby approached her.

"Were you ever scared of becoming a mum?"

Nova was startled by the question. She opened her mouth to deny this but then stopped. Carefully watching Ruby's eyes, she could see that the answer to this question really mattered.

Nova said quietly, honestly. "Sometimes, I still am."

Ruby walked over and sat on the step, looking up at Nova waiting for her to continue.

"When I found out that I was pregnant with Lily, I nearly didn't keep her. Not because I wouldn't love her. I just didn't think I could do it." Nova's voice wobbled slightly. "The truth actually was that her father was already showing signs being unpredictable. I didn't know if it was the right time to have a child."

Ruby watched Daisy and Asha as they trotted happily together towards the house. Both wagging tails. "Lily is amazing." Ruby reflected. "She's so full of laughter and creative ideas for dressing up herself, and any person or dog who comes into her orbit."

Nova smiled warmly. "She fills my heart with so much joy. I can't imagine not having her in my life."

Ruby didn't need to unpack her thoughts with Nova. Just being here and looking at the reminders of Lily everywhere showed her how large was the space that Lily had created in Nova's life. She hadn't shrunk Nova's options. She'd grown them.

Nova stood and offered Ruby some lunch. Ruby, watching Asha and Daisy chasing each other's tails, thought she wouldn't mind sitting for a while amongst Lily's paintings and latest creations, so followed Nova inside.

***

Later, as Ruby was strolling with Asha back across the bridge towards the café, Joe stopped in his ute to ask how her day was going.

"I'm going to tell your boss that she needs to work her slaves a bit harder."

Ruby leaned into the cab and gave his shoulder a playful shove.

"I was given the day off to kick back and rest in the sunshine."

Joe rolled his eyes. "I think I need to change employers. Do you want to jump in and help me deliver a lamb? The ewe's having trouble."

Ruby considered this. "Is it going to be gross? Like, blood and muck?"

"Possibly," Joe acknowledged. "Real life isn't always pretty."

Ruby didn't have any plans for the rest of the afternoon, so she ushered Asha back towards the café when they came to the front of the property, and hopped in the ute with Joe. He filled her in on the farm they were visiting, explaining that it was unusual for a lamb to be born at this time of year. Joe talked about the gestation period of ewes being only five months and that sometimes farmers breed their stock to have autumn lambs, so they spread out the workload across the year.

When they pulled up near the barn, and Joe had jumped out to greet Trevor the farmer, they then walked in to see the ewe having trouble giving birth. Ruby watched with fascination as Joe put on gloves and carefully assessed to find out the position the lamb was sitting in, before guiding it with his hand to gently pull the lamb out.

Ruby hardly noticed the blood, or the mess. All she saw was the tiny little life emerging, wet and still. Ruby stopped breathing as she stared at the lifeless body.

Joe cleared the lamb's airway and rubbed it carefully.

The lamb gasped its first breath.

So did Ruby.

The sound broke something open in her.

She swallowed hard, steadying herself.

Eventually, Ruby said, "You're so gentle with all the animals you work with."

"That's because they can't ask for help. You have to look closely to see what they need. That kind of care … it shapes something in you too." Joe then looked up and smiled at her. "You already know that Rubes, because you have been doing it every day for the past month as you've looked after Ember."

Ruby smiled at the nickname only Joe was allowed to use.

"I can't keep him much longer."

It took Joe a moment to realise Ruby was talking about the joey.

"Yes," Joe sighed, "he'll need to be released to the animal sanctuary soon so he can learn to get along with other wallabies."

"My room will be a bit lonely without him." Ruby already felt the loss.

"Three in one room's plenty, if you count Asha too."

Ruby opened her mouth to say she hadn't decided about the baby yet. But the words didn't come. Because somewhere between Eve's garden, Lily's paintings, and the lamb's first breath ... she already had.

***

Hope stood barefoot at the kitchen bench in the cottage, pouring hot water into a teapot. She hadn't expected company, but when she turned and saw Ruby hovering in the doorway, arms folded, wearing a jumper over pyjamas and Ugg boots, she didn't say anything. Hope just reached for a second mug.

"Couldn't sleep?" She asked gently.

Ruby shrugged and came to sit at the table. "Too many thoughts."

Hope brought over the tea and sat across from her. The light was low, just the little lamp on the shelf by the window casting a warm, golden circle between them.

For a while, they sipped in silence. Then Ruby spoke, her voice low.

"I was pregnant once before. I didn't keep it."

Hope didn't flinch. She just exhaled softly and placed a steady hand on Ruby's arm, waiting.

Then Ruby said quietly, "This time, I want to try something different."

Hope only nodded gently, encouraging Ruby to continue.

"I talked to Eve today. And Nova. And Joe, actually." She stared down into her cup. "It's like I was asking everyone else to give me an answer I already knew."

Hope didn't interrupt. She just waited.

"I think … I want to keep it," Ruby said. The words trembled, but didn't break. "Not because it's easy. Or because I'm ready. But because … it's alive … and might have a great life … that I don't want him or her to miss out on."

Hope's breath caught in her chest. She reached out and placed a hand over Ruby's, just resting there, steady.

"Then we'll figure it out," she said quietly. "Together."

Ruby gave a small, shaky laugh. "I still don't know what that's even going to look like."

"You don't have to," Hope said. "Not tonight. You just have to rest in the decision you've made and know you're not alone in it."

Ruby nodded. Her eyes shimmered, but she didn't cry. Instead, she looked down and placed a hand gently on her belly.

"It's weird. I used to think this meant the end of everything." She glanced up. "But maybe … it's actually the start of something else."

Hope smiled, soft and sure. "It sounds like a weight you've been carrying has been lifted."

Ruby snorted and gave a half-laugh. "Well, I'm pretty sure there's going to be plenty of weight gain ahead."

They sat for a while longer, the silence not heavy now, but filled with a fragile kind of peace. When Ruby finally stood to go back to bed, she paused at the front door and looked back.

"Thanks for not pushing me," she said. "For letting me get there on my own."

Hope gave a quiet nod. "That's what love does."

Ruby didn't answer, but when she left, the way she closed the door behind her was different. Quiet. Reverent.

Almost like she was saying, *Amen.*

CHAPTER 23

S he felt vulnerable tonight. Her polite smile was hiding bruised faith.

She had been to Bible study groups many years ago. Before the betrayal.

Now, she carried questions she didn't dare name aloud.

Just as she reached for the door, it opened from the inside.

Hanna stood there, clutching a small plate of homemade biscuits, her face lighting up in quiet surprise. "Hello, Hope. I saw you coming, and thought I'd welcome you at the door. I didn't know you would be here."

Hope managed a nervous smile. "Neither did I, really."

Hanna stepped aside, holding the door open for her. "Well, then we are both brave tonight."

There was something in her tone, light, but genuine, that settled Hope just a little. Hanna had been in the café a few times lately before opening her florist's shop for the day, curious about everything from macadamias to finger limes. She always asked thoughtful questions and never was in a rush to leave.

They stepped inside together.

"Hope! You made it," Eve said warmly, standing to greet her with a gentle smile. She wore a soft knitted jumper over faded fitted jeans and carried a worn leather Bible tucked under one arm. "Come and sit wherever you like, love."

Nova waved her and Hanna over. Edith gave Hope a smile that reached down inside her like a hug. Some of these women knew Hope and cared about her.

"Hi Hope," chirped Georgia, flashing a bright, polished smile. She sat close to Suzanne and Emma, all three of them looking as if they'd come straight from well-kept homes and tidy routines. Their open Bibles were colour-coded with highlighters and tabs.

Hope had only met these women in brief chats after church and didn't know anything about their families or lives.

Hope smiled a polite greeting, and took a seat beside Nova, grateful for the soft nudge of solidarity.

Eve opened with prayer, simple, and sincere. Then she sat and glanced around the circle.

"Today, I felt led to talk about forgiveness," she said. "Not as a rulebook. Not as a guilt trip. But as something deeper. Something that brings freedom and requires wisdom."

She opened her Bible.

"Forgiveness is something Jesus talked about often. Not as an optional extra, but as a vital part of following Him."

She read softly,

"For if you forgive other people when they sin against you, your heavenly Father will also forgive you. But if you do not forgive others their sins, your Father will not forgive your sins."

There was a stillness in the room. Eve let the words breathe.

She looked up. "That's from Matthew 6:14–15. Depending on the situation you're facing, that can be a difficult teaching to hear. In Ephesians

4:32, Paul writes, '*Be kind and compassionate to one another, forgiving each other, just as in Christ God forgave you.*'"

Hope shifted in her seat.

"Now," Eve continued, "this can raise a lot of questions. Do we have to forgive everyone? Even people who've hurt us deeply and never say sorry. Even when it still hurts?"

Edith was the first to speak. "We're commanded to. But that doesn't mean it's simple."

Nova added, "Sometimes forgiveness feels impossible, especially when someone doesn't care that they hurt you. But I think it's more about releasing your right to punish them. That you are giving it to God."

Georgia's brow creased. "But doesn't that let them off the hook?"

"Only in our hearts," Eve replied gently. "It doesn't remove consequences. It just keeps bitterness from growing in us."

Hanna, who had been quiet until now, shifted slightly in her seat. Her accent, lightly European, gave her words a gentle weight.

"In my country," she said, "people do not talk about forgiveness easily. We carry things. Long histories. Family feuds. War. Sometimes … unforgiveness becomes part of the culture."

She glanced around the group, thoughtful. "When I first came to faith, I was told to forgive everything immediately, because God had forgiven me. And yes, this is beautiful. But I was confused. I did not understand how to forgive and also protect my heart."

She looked over at Hope, then back to Eve. "I think … forgiveness without wisdom can become another kind of harm. I have had to learn that it is not un-Christian to have boundaries. That sometimes love says: I release you to God … but I do not let you stay close."

Hanna paused, then continued. "A boundary isn't always a wall though; it can have a door with a lock. You don't slam it in hate, but you keep it closed until, or unless, it's safe again."

A few women blinked, absorbing her honesty.

Nova nodded slowly. "That's really helpful. It's like we all grew up being taught the what of forgiveness, but not the how."

Hope sat with a burning question she hadn't meant to ask, until it burst out. "Is there ever something that is unforgiveable?"

There was a pause, until Edith quietly said, "Jesus forgave the people nailing Him to the cross. They hadn't repented. He said, '*Father, forgive them, for they know not what they do*'."

Nova nodded slowly. "I think forgiveness is more about releasing the grip something has on you. Not pretending it didn't hurt, but letting go of the poison, so it doesn't eat you alive."

Eve gave her a warm smile. "That's right. Forgiveness is a heart posture before God. We don't wait for the other person to earn it. It doesn't mean the wound didn't matter. It means we entrust justice to God.

"What if someone's really dangerous?" Suzanne asked. "Like ... if they've committed a crime, or harmed someone? Surely, it's not wise to forgive and just let them back in like nothing has happened?"

"Absolutely not," Eve said gently but firmly. "Forgiveness is *not* the same as trust. Forgiveness is a gift we give with God's help. It's such an important concept that, before we move on, we are going to read some other Bible passages on forgiveness and chat about them."

She handed around a page of printed verses.

"Would it help if we broke into two smaller groups to reflect together?" she asked.

Hope felt wary. This might involve more personal sharing than she was ready for.

But Eve glanced her way and added, "Would you like to sit with Edith and Nova?"

Hope nodded, and some of the tension in her chest eased. No difficult questions. No judgement. Just two women who knew her story and had stayed in relationship with her.

***

A while later, Eve asked the women to gather back together again.

She returned to Suzanne's earlier question. "We've been talking about forgiveness. But does forgiving someone mean that we have to trust them again?"

Eve passed around a second handout.

"God's Word is our source of wisdom in relationships," she said. "God asks us to trust Him, because he is always faithful and trustworthy. But people aren't always safe. They're not always trustworthy. And trust isn't automatically restored when we forgive someone."

Eve paused, letting the room settle.

"For trust to be rebuilt, there must be repentance. If a relationship has been broken by sin or harm, restoration can only happen where there's repentance, and real change demonstrated over time, not just words."

Hope stared at the Bible verses on the page.

Luke 13:3 – "*Unless you repent, you too will all perish.*"

Acts 3:19 – "*Repent and turn to God, so that your sins may be wiped out.*"

Eve continued, "We often feel pressure to 'move on' or 'be nice', especially in church settings. But Scripture doesn't ask us to ignore sin. In fact, it calls us to lovingly confront it."

She read aloud, *"If someone sins against you, go and show them their fault. If they listen, you've won them back. But if not … you treat them as a Gentile or a tax collector."*

Eve looked up. "That's Matthew 18. Jesus isn't telling us to give up on people, but He's reminding us that repentance matters. Without it, trust can't be restored."

Emma stirred. "So, forgiveness is about the heart … but trust depends on behaviour?"

"Exactly," Eve said. "You can forgive someone completely, with God's help, and still choose to maintain distance. If someone has caused deep harm, and shows no change, you can still say, 'I forgive you … but I don't feel safe being in a relationship with you.' That's not a lack of faith. That's wisdom and stewardship of your own well-being."

Georgia shifted in her chair, uncomfortable with where this discussion was headed. "So, we're saying it's okay to forgive, but still walk away from relationships?"

Eve responded. "Every situation is unique and different, and God is powerful, so if people submit to Him, hearts and lives can be changed." But then continued gently, "However, in some situations, when harm continues and there's no repentance or willingness to change, it may be no longer wise or safe to stay in the relationship. Forgiveness is always something God calls us to grow in, but restoration requires both hearts to be open to Him. It requires people to be truthful about any harm they have caused, to apologise, and be willing to be accountable as they demonstrate changed behaviour."

Emma frowned faintly. "But shouldn't we stay? I mean, God doesn't want us to walk out on relationship commitments." Her fingers traced the edge of her Bible. She wasn't arguing exactly, just struggling to reconcile everything she'd been taught.

Emma's words echoed what others in the circle had been told before, that hope, and following God's teachings, meant forgiving and staying in relationships no matter the cost.

Eve nodded slowly. "Yes. We always hope that God will convict or soften people's hearts. But God requires authentic repentant hearts for reconciliation and restoration. As Hanna shared with us earlier, with people who aren't repentant, and don't have any willingness to change, we need boundaries. They aren't bitterness. They're wisdom. They protect your life while you wait to see whether trust can be safely rebuilt. And in some cases, wisdom might mean letting God work in that person's life from a distance."

Eve glanced around the group, voice calm but firm. "Sometimes, the most loving thing we can do is forgive without being close to someone. You can forgive and still walk in truth from a distance. You can hope and still hold a boundary. These aren't signs of weak faith, they're signs of wisdom."

A deep quiet fell over the room.

Eve let it linger. Then she said softly, "Ask God to show you where you're holding pain … where He's prompting you to forgive … and where you may need to wait, or step back, while He works in someone else's heart. James 1:5 reminds us that if we need wisdom, we should ask God, '*who gives generously to all without reproach*.'"

Hope felt something uncoil in her chest, a thread of tension she hadn't even realised she'd been carrying. All those years, people at church had told her to try harder in her marriage, to be more patient. Of being told to pray more. To forgive and forget.

Maybe … that was never what God had asked of her.

Eve closed the study with a question.

"Who do you need to forgive, with God's help?"

The room was still. No pressure. Just reflection.

For once, Hope didn't feel judged by the quiet.

She felt understood.

As the others slowly rose to pack up, Georgia leaned toward Emma and murmured, "I don't know ... sometimes it feels like people give up on grace too quickly."

Hope caught the whisper, but didn't react.

She just closed her Bible and stood.

Nova placed a warm hand on her back.

"Don't worry," Nova murmured. "God knows our stories."

As Hope gathered her things, Hanna stepped beside her, tucking a loose strand of hair behind her ear.

"I liked what you said," Hanna said softly. "About wondering if some things are unforgiveable. I have wondered too."

Hope glanced over, surprised. "You have?"

Hanna nodded. "Yes. But I think God can hold our questions. Even the ones we're too afraid to say out loud."

She smiled, gently. "I think He is more patient with our pain than people often are."

Hope pressed her Bible to her chest before sliding it into her bag. Something in her felt steadier than when she'd walked in.

God knew her whole story. She didn't need to explain anything to Him. He'd walked through it with her.

CHAPTER 24

It was Monday afternoon. Ruby stood at the edge of the café garden, cradling the pouch tight against her chest. Ember stirred, his dark eyes blinking up at her, unaware that today was goodbye. She had spent the past five weeks loving and nurturing him, and didn't know if she could now let go.

"He's ready," Joe said quietly, holding the travel crate in one hand.

Ruby nodded. Her throat felt tight. "I know. I just … I don't think I can watch him hop away."

Hope stepped forward. "You've given him such an amazing start in life, love. Letting go of those we care for at the right time is part of loving well."

Ruby looked at her, then at Joe, and gave a small, brave nod. "You two can take him. Tell him I said goodbye." She whispered. "And to be brave."

She pressed her face briefly into the soft fur, breathing in his earthy warmth before passing him to Joe. She then turned and walked quickly towards the café before they could see the tears spill over.

***

The road to the animal sanctuary curved along dry ridges and burnt-out patches still recovering from the fire. Hope sat in the passenger seat, her hands resting in her lap.

"Ruby did the right thing," Joe said, after a long silence. "Sometimes we can only allow growth to happen when we let go. Love comes with so many different challenges."

Hope glanced at him. "Sometimes, it requires us surviving after it's gone."

Joe's brow furrowed. "That comment you made after church the other week … about not being supported in your faith community … I've been meaning to ask, what did that look like for you? If it's not too much to share."

Hope hesitated. "It's hard to explain. I think … I learned to make myself small, even in church. Mark was charming to everyone else, so when I did speak up, people thought I was exaggerating or being overly sensitive. That I just needed to pray more, submit more."

Joe didn't speak, just kept his eyes on the road.

"Mark grew up in a house full of chaos. His mum screamed and twisted everything into guilt. His dad drank himself into quiet. I only met them a couple of times, but the pain was obvious. Mark never talked about it. He just … tried to control everything he could. Including me."

Hope paused and swallowed down emotions before continuing. "I think this was part of why I stayed for so long when the relationship became unhealthy and dangerous. I thought I could help him. I felt responsible for helping to save him. But I only realised at the end, that was never my job."

"Control hides fear," Joe said gently. "And shame."

She nodded. "But he never owned it. Just told me I was the weak one."

Joe's voice was low. "Maybe standing over you felt like he wasn't beneath everyone else."

The only noise for the next few minutes was the quiet hum of tyres on gravel.

"My dad drank too," Joe said after careful consideration. "But Mum was the anchor. She was gentle, but resilient. She had a deep and genuine faith. I don't remember Dad being abusive … but he didn't step up … or help out."

He glanced at her. "I reckon that made the difference for me, though. I saw what *not* to be, and someone strong enough to show me there was another way. I was also blessed to have a godly, wise, and faithful grandad who showed me what it looked like as a man to be strong and care for others."

Hope felt her breath catch. Not because he'd said something grand, but because he hadn't.

Shared wisdom. No performance. No posturing. Just truth.

"Thank you," she said softly. "For listening … and sharing with me."

"Anytime." A small smile. "I'm planning to be here in town for the long haul."

Hope wrestled with what she wanted to say. Eventually she spoke. "My heart's still so bruised. I live with fear … and trusting others doesn't come easily. But being here in Wombat Valley is giving me the time and space to heal. I am so thankful for what feels like a second chance. Not just at life, but in knowing what it means to feel safe again … even if I do check over my shoulder sometimes."

Joe didn't reply. But slowly reached across the space between them and held her hand. Just for a moment. Giving it a quick squeeze by way of acknowledgement.

Hope smiled at him, their eyes meeting in quiet understanding.

She then looked out at the smoke-silvered bushland as they neared the sanctuary. The world was still healing. It was scorched but slowly greening again. Maybe she was too.

***

They pulled up at the edge of the sanctuary, where the bushland stretched out like a scar stitched with green. It was quiet, just the faint rustle of leaves and the distant warble of magpies.

Joe carried the crate through the gate while Hope followed, their boots crunching on the dry earth. Ahead, a volunteer greeted them and opened the gate on the securely fenced enclosure, stepping back with a nod as they walked inside.

Joe knelt and unlatched the crate. Ember hesitated, then leapt.

Not far. Just a few tentative hops, his ears twitching, head turning as if unsure of this wide world. Then another bound. And another.

"There he goes," Joe murmured. "Braver than he knows."

Hope echoed Ruby's farewell. "Goodbye, little one. You have been dearly loved. We hope your life is full and long."

Hope watched him disappear behind some upright hollow logs which the volunteers had placed fresh grass bunches and soft hay in for feeding. She then noticed another joey hop in the same direction. A gust of wind carried the scent of eucalyptus and ash.

She knelt briefly, brushing her hand over the scorched ground. The soil was dry and crumbling, but something green pressed up through the ash beside her fingers—a stubborn little shoot.

"It's strange," she said quietly. "How something can look burned out ... but still hold life underneath."

Joe didn't respond right away. He just stepped up beside her, then spoke. "That's how healing works. It takes time. Doesn't always look like much at first."

Walking back to the car, Hope thought about the ways she was seeing evidence of healing in her own life.

***

As they drove away, Hope watched the sanctuary disappear in the rearview mirror. Ember was already a memory tucked into the curve of the land. She felt lighter somehow. Not fixed, not finished. But freer.

Yet just as they turned the bend onto the main road, the dark clouds shifted across the setting sun, casting them into sudden gloom. Joe flicked the headlights on.

Hope didn't speak, but her fingers curled slightly in her lap.

Something stirred beneath her peace.

Not fear, just unease.

The kind that whispers a reminder: not all goodbyes stay gone.

CHAPTER 25

Hope carried a mug of herbal tea out the front to Ruby, who was crouched by the chalkboard, writing in her boldest script:

Gone to Church — Open at 12 Noon :)

Hope smiled faintly. "Think the smiley face will make the coffee crowd more forgiving?"

Ruby grinned. "Definitely."

Rowena emerged from the kitchen, wiping her hands on a tea towel. "Why are you closing this morning? I usually open up for your Sunday morning regulars."

Hope shrugged. "Just for a couple of hours. It might nudge a few of them to think about coming along. They may find it good for the soul, it seems to keep Ruby out of mischief."

"I heard that," Ruby said, still crouched.

"You were meant to," Hope replied, flicking her playfully with a tea towel.

Ruby stood and dusted her hands. "You should come with us today, Row."

Rowena raised an eyebrow. "To church?"

"Yes," Hope said seizing the moment. "You've been working hard all week. Come sit, sing a few songs, breathe in something good. We can grab seats up the back."

Rowena sighed. "Fine. I can come along to try it as a once off. But only if you promise I don't have to sing."

"You can mime," Ruby offered. "God will understand."

Hope turned to head back inside and make a coffee for Row.

Just then, a man crossed the road and paused to glance at the chalkboard. He gave a small nod of amusement and kept walking, wearing neat jeans, a collared shirt, and looking a bit too dressed up for a Sunday café regular.

"That fellow's been in a few times," Rowena called inside to Hope, watching him disappear down the street. "Usually on Sundays after you've headed off to church. Said he's passing through but seemed real interested in the café. He asked all sorts of questions. Said his name was Jamie."

When Hope returned outside she looked but could only see the man's retreating back in the distance. "What kind of questions?"

"Oh, you know. How long we've been open, who owns it, how the renovations came about. He seemed chatty and polite."

There was a pause.

Rowena glanced sideways. "Why? Something wrong?"

Hope forced a smile. "No. Just curious."

The women soon ducked inside to finish setting the tables, getting everything ready for the lunch crowd after church.

A few minutes later, Ruby unfastened her apron. "Alright. God's waiting."

They laughed together as they locked the door, the café still warm with morning life.

As Hope walked toward the car, she glanced back once over her shoulder.

The man was gone.

***

Hope, Ruby and Rowena stood in the back row as the congregation rose to sing the final song. A few people near the front were still seated as Hope glanced ahead, then she saw a man turn to speak to the person beside him.

Her heart stopped.

It was Mark.

A wave of nausea rolled through her, rising like bile in her throat.

Rowena, following her gaze, smiled and whispered, "There's that lovely guy, Jamie, I told you about, who comes in on Sunday mornings. He always asks after you, actually."

Hope's body stiffened. Her breath came too fast.

She turned abruptly to Ruby. "I'm not feeling well. I need to go ... now."

Ruby blinked. "Want me to come?"

Hope shook her head, barely able to speak. "No. Stay. I just ... I need air."

She slipped into the aisle and out the door just as the congregation began to sing:

"Bless the Lord, O my soul ..."

Joe, still up the front with his guitar, saw her leave. His brow creased in concern.

Hope reached the car with trembling fingers and sat behind the wheel, staring through the windscreen. She couldn't go back. Couldn't think. Couldn't breathe. She needed space. Time to breathe and understand what she'd just seen.

He was here. In her church. Using a new name. Wearing the same old lies.

She grabbed her phone and typed quickly:

"Ruby and Row, sorry. Can you both cover lunch today? I'm not well enough to work."

Then she started the engine and drove.

**

The final song faded. Pastor Tom led the benediction before dismissing the congregation with a gentle encouragement to stay for coffee and conversation together outside.

As people turned to greet one another, Mark stood from his seat near the front. He clapped Steve lightly on the back, then turned to a man across the aisle with a warm smile and handshake.

"Good to be here," he said. "Such a grounded, welcoming church."

Joe stepped down from the front and crossed paths with him near the doors.

"Hey there," Joe said, offering a nod. "Don't think we've met."

The man's face lit up with friendly confidence. "Jamie."

Joe shook his hand, noting the firm, practiced grip. "Joe Butler. I saw you walking past the café this morning."

"I've popped into *The Hearth* over a few Sundays," Jamie said easily. "Great place. There's something magnetic about people rebuilding. It draws you in."

Joe offered a polite smile, but the phrasing made something shift in his gut. Rebuilding?

"You, local?" he asked.

"Not exactly," Jamie replied. "Just spending weekends here. Seeking a bit of peace … and trying to reconcile with someone important to me."

Joe's brow furrowed slightly. "They live here?"

Jamie nodded. "Yes. It's complicated. But I've done a lot of personal work. I believe restoration's possible."

Before Joe could respond, Pastor Tom joined them with a warm greeting. "Good Morning. I don't believe we've met."

"Jamie," Mark said smoothly. "Just visiting. Thanks for your message today. The part about mercy not being soft really struck me."

Tom smiled. "God's mercy always costs something. It's never cheap grace."

"Exactly," Jamie said, nodding. "I know what it is to fall short. But I've repented. Fully. I've come to ask forgiveness; from someone I once failed."

Tom paused, something unreadable passing through his gaze.

"Well," he said quietly, "I hope your time here helps bring clarity. And peace, for everyone involved."

Jamie bowed his head slightly. "That's the prayer."

From the other side of the foyer, Steve and Mike appeared.

"There you are!" Steve called. "Mate, you've got to come round for lunch. Emma's cooked up a storm."

Jamie gave a broad smile. "You sure? I don't want to intrude."

"Nonsense," Mike said, already ushering him out the doors. "Think of yourself as one of us."

As the three men disappeared outside, Tom glanced at Joe.

Joe murmured, "Something about him doesn't sit right."

Tom gave a slow nod. "Let's watch. Truth often rises."

***

The smell of roast lamb filled the kitchen as Steve uncorked a bottle of red and offered Mark a glass.

"Not too much," Mark said with an easy smile. "Still getting my bearings out here. Your town's a far cry from the city."

"Ah well," Mike chuckled, "might be sleepy, with more cows, but we have less traffic."

Emma brought out the roast vegetables, setting them on the table. "I'm so glad you could join us, Jamie. It's lovely to meet someone new with such a heart for faith and restoration."

Mark's smile deepened. "Thank you. It's been a long journey to get here. Spiritually and literally."

Mike leaned in. "What brought you out this way?"

Mark paused just long enough to seem humble. "I suppose the short version is … repentance. I made some terrible mistakes. For a long time, I convinced myself I was the victim. But God wouldn't let me stay blind. He brought me to a point where I couldn't ignore my part in what went wrong."

There was a thoughtful silence around the table as cutlery clinked softly against plates.

"Was it a marriage?" Steve asked.

Mark nodded slowly. "Yes. We were young when we got together and full of dreams. But she lost both her parents, and … it broke something in her. She pulled away. Shut down. It was like losing someone who was still right there in the room."

Emma's brow furrowed, quietly sympathetic.

"I did what I could to hold things together," Mark said. "Kept the house together, encouraged her, prayed like mad. But I guess … I also became too directive. I see that now."

Suzanne, who'd been quiet, offered gently, "Grief changes people."

"It does," Mark agreed. "And I didn't handle that well. Eventually, she told people I was emotionally abusive. That I manipulated her faith. That was quite a shock to me … I really did try to help her rely on truth more than emotion. But maybe I went too far. Maybe she wasn't ready to hear it."

Mike shifted, uncertain. Steve nodded quickly.

"That's the thing, mate," Steve said. "Sometimes women get overwhelmed … and misread things. You try to lead, and suddenly you're the bad guy."

Mark gave a careful laugh. "Well … I wouldn't put it like that. But I've learned this, if someone believes they were hurt, you have to take that seriously. Even when their story looks different from your side."

He took a sip of wine and glanced out the window. His tone softened.

"I made a mistake too. Let someone else in. Just emotionally, at first. Then more. And that broke what little was left between us. I carry deep regret over that. But I've ended that relationship. I've repented. I've done counselling. And I've come here … because I want to find her. Ask for forgiveness. Make things right."

Emma hesitated. "What did you say your wife's name was?"

Mark nodded, his expression open and sorrowful. "Hope. Hope Elkins. Though she might use her maiden name now."

Mike and Steve exchanged a look.

"We thought her husband's name was Mark," Mike said.

Mark gave a sheepish smile. "It is. Or was. Mark James Elkins. But I go by Jamie now. It's part of a fresh start. A reminder to myself, and to God, that I'm not the same man."

There was a long pause. Suzanne looked uneasy, but Mike's hand on her arm settled her.

Steve leaned forward, a little too eager. "Well, Jamie, every man's got a past. What matters is what you're doing about it now. A woman gets emotional, tells her side … that can spiral fast. If there's anything we can do to help you reconnect with her, just say the word."

Mark gave a modest nod. "Thank you. That means more than you know."

Emma began clearing plates, slower than usual, her expression unreadable.

Outside, the wind stirred through the gum trees. And somewhere in Steve's backyard, a loose gate banged softly against its frame, the only sound that didn't seem entirely under control.

CHAPTER 26

*H*ope had been driving up to the Southern Highlands, trying to get out of town. To put her out of reach of the man she'd worked so hard to escape.

She was still reeling from shock. Mark had been turning up at her café for weeks on Sunday mornings, when she wasn't there, prying information out of Rowena about her. And now today, he'd been sitting in her church, laughing and chatting at the front like he belonged there.

She didn't know what to do. After months spent building a new life where she'd finally felt safe, all she could think about was running.

Hope couldn't face it all over again. The fear, the manipulation, the unravelling of herself. Last time, it had nearly destroyed her.

As she drove, her mind raced in circles, desperately searching for answers.

Her phone rang, echoing through the car's speaker system.

Joe Butler

Needing to hear a steady voice, Hope answered.

"Hey," Joe said gently. "Ruby told me you left church feeling unwell. She said you looked like you'd seen a ghost."

"I'm okay," she said, her voice flat. "Just … something's happened."

Joe was quiet for a moment. Then, choosing his words carefully, he invited her to trust him. "Hope. You don't have to tell me what's going on. But I care. And I'd rather hear it from you than second-hand."

There was a pause.

"It was him," she said. "Mark. He was there this morning at church. Calling himself Jamie."

"Wait—" Joe sounded stunned. "That was Mark?"

"Jamie ... well James, is his middle name. He's been using it. Apparently, he's been coming into the café too. I had no idea."

"Oh, Hope. I'm so sorry. That must've felt like a punch to the chest."

Joe sounded concerned. "Hope, he's telling people at church that he is here to reconcile your relationship and that he is repentant."

Her voice wavered. "I feel ... completely blindsided. Unsafe."

"You have every right to feel that way."

He hesitated, then added carefully, "But, I need to say something, and I hope you'll understand. While he's in town claiming he wants to restore your marriage ... I'll need to step back a little. Legally, and spiritually, I want to honour your space to make decisions. And I don't want to give him any reason to make accusations about you."

"I understand," she said quietly. She understood but this felt like another shift in a world that no longer felt stable.

His tone softened, but it was still steady. "But know this: if he pressures you in any way, if you ever feel unsafe or threatened, I'll be there in a heartbeat. You are not alone. You don't have to carry this on your own."

Her voice softened too. "Thank you, Joe. That means more than I can say."

"Talk to Eve. Talk to Tom. Don't let him twist the story. And when you're ready, tell your truth."

She thanked him. Before ending the call, he told her he would be praying for her every day.

***

After speaking to Joe, Hope felt the tightness in her chest begin to ease. His calm words, and the reminder to speak with Eve or Tom, grounded her. She wasn't alone. This community had welcomed her with warmth and care, and now, more than ever, she needed to lean on that.

She thought of the compassion Eve had shown during the women's evening for those who'd come from hard places. And without overthinking, Hope tapped the contact and called from the speakerphone.

Eve answered almost immediately.

"Hi Eve. It's Hope. Do you have a few minutes to speak?"

She didn't wait. "Eve … I saw him. Mark. At church. He's calling himself Jamie now. He's telling people he's changed—that he's here to reconcile our marriage."

There was a sharp intake of breath. "Oh, Hope," Eve said. "Are you safe right now?"

"I left straight after the service. I've just been driving. I haven't gone back to the café yet. I feel like … the ground's shifted underneath me."

"That makes complete sense. You've had your peace disrupted," Eve said gently. "And that peace you've been growing, it's a gift from God. What's happening now isn't."

Hope's voice wavered. "He says he's repented. That he wants to restore the marriage. But I don't feel safe. I don't even know what's real."

"Hope, restoration takes more than words. It takes repentance, accountability, and change over time. It's not unloving to be cautious, or to protect yourself."

She paused, her tone gentle. "Psalm 9 says the Lord is a refuge for the oppressed. And Proverbs warns us not to walk closely with those whose ways are destructive. You're not wrong to be wary."

Hope swallowed. "I don't know what he'll be saying to people. He's lied before. Twisted things. I'm scared they'll think I'm bitter, or unforgiving."

"Forgiveness is different to relationship restoration," Eve said quietly. "Trust is earned. And when someone keeps distorting truth or slandering you, it's not safe, or wise, to hand that trust back."

"So … what do I do?"

"Be honest. Stay safe. And if you do speak with him, don't do it alone. Let truth be your covering. And remember, Hope, you're not walking this road alone."

Eve prayed over the phone, asking God to protect Hope, to calm her heart, and to guide her with wisdom. For her to know when to speak and when to remain silent. She read aloud:

"*The Lord is a refuge for the oppressed, a stronghold in times of trouble.*" (Psalm 9:9)

"*I know that the Lord secures justice for the poor and upholds the cause of the needy.*" (Psalm 140:12)

"Amen," Hope whispered as they ended the call.

***

The late afternoon sun spilled gold across the floorboards as Hope stepped back into *The Hearth*. The lunch rush had passed, and a calm stillness filled the space. It was the kind of hush that lingers after a day that held more than it first revealed.

Rowena looked up from wiping down the counter, pausing mid-motion. Ruby stood nearby, stacking clean mugs.

"There you are," Rowena said gently. "You, okay?"

Hope gave a small nod and pulled her jacket closer around her. "Getting there."

Ruby crossed the room and wrapped her in a quick hug. "You scared us this morning. You looked like you'd seen a ghost."

Hope let out a long breath, steadying herself. "It was Mark."

Rowena's hand froze on the cloth. "What?"

Hope nodded. "Mark James Elkins. He's been using his middle name."

Silence fell, sharp and heavy.

Ruby pulled back, eyes wide. "He was at church?"

"Yes. And apparently, he's also been in here the last few Sundays, talking to Rowena. Asking about the café restoration. About me."

Rowena's face went pale. "Hope, I didn't know. He just seemed … curious. Friendly. Said he was passing through. I never would have—"

"It's okay," Hope said gently, lifting a hand. "You couldn't have known. He's good at that."

Ruby folded her arms. "Jamie … Mark … came in after church today too. Asked if you were around. Said he was heading back to the city but would be back next weekend."

Hope blinked. "He's coming back?"

Ruby nodded. "That's what he said."

A pause.

Then Rowena straightened and said, "Well. Let him come. We'll be ready for him."

Hope raised an eyebrow.

"We're not afraid of him," Rowena added. "And you don't have to face him alone."

Ruby was already nodding. "Exactly. You've got us. And if needed, I'm sure others in town will stand with you too."

A lump formed in Hope's throat, emotion rising at their quiet solidarity.

"I don't want to hide," she said softly. "I don't want to cower like I used to. We've been planning the school fete stall next weekend, and I'm not going to let him scare me out of showing up."

"Good," Ruby said. "Because we'll be right there beside you. He won't know what hit him."

Rowena nodded, eyes fierce. "I reckon that man's got no idea who he's dealing with now."

Hope let out a soft laugh, the first real one all day.

She looked around *The Hearth*, at the café that had become her place of renewal. Then she looked at the two women beside her. Steady. Strong.

She wasn't alone.

CHAPTER 27

The morning air held the bite of autumn, sharp and edged with heavy mist. Hope stood in the driveway next to *The Hearth*, balancing towers of takeaway soup cups in a box while Ruby and Rowena loaded the last batch of foil-wrapped pizza trays into the car.

The school fête had always been a highlight on Wombat Valley's calendar. But this year, it meant more than that. It was a symbol of recovery after the fire, and a way to give back and come together. The school's decision to donate all proceeds to WIRES had stirred something in people. Everyone, from the mechanic to the florist, had donated something. Even the children had painted river stones as animals to sell. Lily had reported this to them with wide-eyed enthusiasm.

Hope tightened her grip on the tray. She'd told herself she was going. She was showing up. But now, as the car tailgate closed and Ruby passed her a coffee to go, her hands trembled slightly.

"You, okay?" Ruby asked, watching her.

Hope nodded, then exhaled. "More nerves than I expected."

Rowena grinned as she started the engine. "It's only soup and pizza, love. Not MasterChef."

Hope gave a half-smile. "It's not the food I'm nervous about."

They all knew what she meant. But no one said his name.

Rowena reached for her seatbelt. "We'll head over there together. I will come back later if we need more."

Hope slipped into the front seat beside her. The café disappeared in the rear-view mirror as they pulled out onto the road. Hope glanced at some roadside trees beginning to resprout after the fire. Life, rising from the ash.

She whispered a quiet prayer as they crossed the bridge toward the school:

Lord, help me to stand. Help me to lean on you.

***

The scent of sizzling sausages and woodfired pizza drifted on the breeze as the school oval buzzed with life. Colourful bunting flapped around the sporting posts, children dashed between cake stalls and face painting, and someone had set up a hay bale obstacle course near the playground.

Hope stood behind her stall beneath a cheerful sign Ruby had made:

The Hearth Café — Soul-Warming Soup & Pizza Slices

A steady stream of parents and kids passed by, waving, chatting, and gratefully collecting lunch in compostable cups and cardboard trays. Beside her, as she popped pre-cooked pizza slices into their small portable ovens, Rowena handled the cash box, while Ruby ladled soup from the slow cookers into steaming cups like a professional.

Hope brushed a loose strand of hair from her face and took a moment to breathe it in: the colour, the noise, and the warmth of community life. This was what she'd dreamed of when she first reopened the café. And somehow, despite recent events, she was still here. Still standing.

A group of children ran past with paper animal masks flapping on their faces. One of them, Nova's little Lily, paused at their stall. "I can buy soup for wombats," she declared solemnly, holding up a gold coin.

Hope leaned down. "That's very generous of you Lily. I'm sure they'd love it … if wombats ate soup."

Lily giggled and dashed off again with her school friends.

"Look at this turnout," Rowena said, passing over change to a pair of teenagers. "I reckon half the town's here."

More than half, Hope thought. Nearly the whole town had turned up. She scanned the crowd automatically, still alert and still braced, but so far, there was no sign of Mark.

Instead, she spotted Joe at the WIRES information booth, crouched beside a crate. A cluster of children leaned in as he gently lifted a sleepy young wombat wrapped in a towel. The animal blinked slowly in the bright light, then settled back down against his chest.

"Little guy's a natural showstopper," Ruby murmured, following her gaze. "Joe could charge admission for cuddles."

Hope smiled. The sight of him surrounded by children and animals, patient and quiet, brought a warmth that settled in her chest.

Just then, Edith and Rob approached the stall, each carrying a small plate of scones teetering with jam and cream. Rob leaned over the table. "Your pizza's better than the one from the bakery stall. Don't tell Clare I said that."

"We'll take that as a high compliment," Hope replied.

Rob looked at Hope kindly. "You've done well, love. It's good to see you here."

Hope nodded, swallowing the emotion that rose unexpectedly in her throat.

***

Emma stood beside the animal themed cake competition table, arms folded, and brow furrowed. "I still think we should talk to her."

Suzanne handed her a paper plate with some carrot cake. "Now's not the time. Look at her, she's up to her elbows in soup and smiling happily for the first time in months."

"But don't you think she deserves to know what he said?"

Suzanne sighed. "What exactly did he say, Em?"

Emma lowered her voice. "Just that he was here to make things right. That he's changed. He talked about her being an emotional wreck and accusing him of things he hadn't done. He said he's forgiven her."

Suzanne looked out across the crowd. "I did hear him say that at lunch … but it sounds like only words with no action … like someone who has caused harm but hasn't actually apologised or made things right."

Emma hesitated. "But what if some of what he's saying is true? What if he's not as bad as we've been told. What if he really has changed?"

Suzanne turned to face her. "Then that truth will still be true tomorrow. And the next day. He can prove that over time. Without causing more pain."

Emma's mouth opened, then closed again.

A few metres away, Hope was laughing with a little boy whose cup of soup had nearly tipped over. Ruby caught it just in time and gave him a high-five.

Suzanne nodded toward the scene. "That woman has rebuilt her life from the ground up. If Mark's had a change of heart, great. But it doesn't mean he gets to walk back in and rewrite the story."

Emma looked uncertain. "I just hate feeling caught in the middle."

"Yes," Suzanne said, her voice gentler. "But we don't know the truth of what has really happened. Sometimes the loving thing isn't stepping in to take sides. It's holding your tongue and letting people who do have more knowledge—or the skills to find the truth—offer support."

A loud cheer erupted near the sack race line as Craig tripped over a hay bale. Nova was standing nearby and stepped forward to check he was okay. Both women turned, laughing, and the tension eased for a moment.

But Emma's eyes drifted back to the soup stall.

"I just hope it doesn't all blow up and become ugly."

***

The lull while the races were on gave Hope a moment to breathe. A breeze rustled through the nearby trees, and somewhere a child shrieked with delight at winning a sack race ribbon. Ruby was restocking soup cups; Rowena had left to go and prepare some more pizzas at the café to bring back.

As Hope handed a soup cup to a young boy with a toothless grin, she glanced up and saw Hanna approaching, tucking a scarf tighter around her neck. Her cheeks were flushed from the cool breeze, and she carried a couple of cinnamon doughnuts in one napkined hand.

"Your stall smells like a feast," she said with a smile, her accent warm and melodic. "Pumpkin soup … it reminds me of home. Not the food, but the feeling."

Hope gave a small, grateful smile. "Thank you. It's been a good day. Mostly."

Hanna tilted her head slightly, as if reading beyond the words. "I heard … that you might be keeping an eye out for someone who isn't safe." She didn't say Mark's name. Didn't need to.

Hope looked down, fiddling with a spoon. "People are talking."

"Yes," Hanna said simply. "But God listens. And He knows who's telling the truth."

Hope met her eyes, surprised by the certainty in them.

Hanna leaned closer, her voice low. "Back in Bible study, you asked if some things were unforgiveable. I've been thinking about that. And I don't know all the answers yet, but … I think God does not ask us to pretend that wolves are sheep."

Hope blinked, her breath catching.

She let this truth sink in.

Hanna smiled gently. "Forgiveness is not the same as forgetting how to make sure you are safe."

There was no pity in her voice. Just quiet, lived-in wisdom.

Hope nodded slowly. "Thank you."

Hanna shrugged one shoulder. "You are showing up. That's brave. Not everyone does that."

She offered one of her remaining doughnuts to Ruby, gave Hope's arm a gentle squeeze, and moved off toward the cake stall without ceremony.

Hope turned back toward the table just as Joe stepped up to the front of the stall, wiping his hands on a cloth and smiling at her in that quiet, steady way of his.

"Any soup left for a hungry vet?" he asked.

"Always," Hope said, reaching for the ladle. "Pumpkin or tomato and basil?"

"Pumpkin. The wombat voted for it."

She smiled, pouring the bright orange soup into a cup and topping it with a sprinkle of fresh herbs.

Joe handed over a few gold coins. "You've had a good crowd today."

"It's been steady. Nice to be part of it."

He took the soup and held it for a moment, then said, "I admire you coming today, Hope. Considering the situation, that shows real bravery. More than most people will ever realise."

His words were simple, but they landed deep. Hope met his gaze, steady and warm. "Thank you. I almost didn't."

Joe nodded. "I figured. But you did."

Their eyes met again, and this time the silence between them said more than words. Hope felt herself steady a little more inside.

He took a sip of the soup. "This is really good, by the way."

"Ruby made it."

"Tell her she's hired."

He gave a quick smile and held her gaze for a moment before turning to walk back toward the WIRES stall, where a group of children were now clustered around a basket lined with towels.

Hope watched him go, then turned back to her counter.

She wasn't doing this alone.

***

The café was still and warm when Rowena came out from the storeroom with more soup to defrost. The oven hummed gently, and the scent of melted cheese and tomato lingered in the air. She moved quickly, pulling on a pair of mitts and sliding a tray of fresh pizzas onto the cooling rack.

The first batch was already boxed. She was reaching for another box to fold when the bell above the front door tinkled.

Rowena looked up and froze.

Footsteps, slow and confident, crossed the timber floor toward the counter.

She stood with the kind of calm she reserved for broken glass.

Mark Elkins stood in front of the till, casual as anything, hands in his jacket pockets, smiling like he owned the place.

"Rowena." he said, voice smooth. "I was hoping to catch up with you."

Rowena didn't return the smile. "You have."

He nodded toward the empty café. "Quiet day?"

"We're at the school fête," she said. "I'm just preparing some more food to take over."

"Ah." He looked pleased with himself. "So, Hope's there too?"

Rowena's expression didn't shift. "She's busy running the stall. It's been full-on."

"Right." He glanced around the café again, then back to her. "I just wanted to speak to her. No drama. I'm not here to stir anything up."

Rowena didn't reply.

He tried again. "I know I'm not her favourite person these days. But people can change."

She met his gaze squarely. "Maybe. But you don't get to decide how, or when, someone else forgives you."

Mark's smile faltered.

"I'd suggest giving her space," Rowena added. "She's doing really well here."

His expression tightened just slightly. "I'm not the enemy, you know."

Rowena reached for the pizza boxes. "Then don't act like it."

Mark opened his mouth as if to speak, but Rowena was already turning back toward the kitchen.

"You'll have to excuse me," she said. "These pizzas won't prepare themselves."

She didn't look back as she went into the kitchen. The tray in her hands trembled just slightly, but her jaw was set.

By the time she carried the boxes out to the car, Mark was nowhere in sight.

***

The afternoon sun had almost disappeared by the time the school grounds began to quieten. Children's helium balloons fluttered in the breeze, and the crowd had thinned to clusters of families lingering over the last of the cakes and those enjoying the final minutes of the petting zoo.

Hope was wiping down the folding table when she spotted Tom and Eve approaching. They walked slowly, hand in hand, pausing now and then to greet people along the way. Tom wore a peaked flat cap; Eve had an insulated coffee mug in her hand and a gentle smile on her face.

Hope stood a little straighter as they reached the stall.

"You've had a big day," Tom said, looking around at the empty trays and soup pots.

"We made it through," Hope said with a smile. "Just don't ask how many pizzas we've served."

Eve stepped forward and offered her a warm hug. "We saw you laughing earlier, with the little crowd of children wearing wombat masks."

Hope gave a small nod. "Today's been … good. A bit strange, but much better than I expected."

Tom's eyes crinkled. "Strange is where grace often shows up."

Hope smiled softly, then glanced around. "Mark didn't come."

Eve didn't respond straight away. She reached into her bag and handed Hope a small, folded note with something scribbled on it.

"Isaiah 41:10," she said gently. "We read it this morning. It reminded me of you."

Hope unfolded the paper. The verse Eve had written was simple, but it stilled something inside her:

"*Do not fear, for I am with you; be not dismayed for I am your God. I will strengthen you and help you; I will uphold you with my righteous right hand.*"

Tom rested a hand on the table. "Hope, you've shown up today with courage and grace. Don't listen to or be distracted by gossip, your life is speaking truth."

Hope blinked back sudden tears.

"We're praying for you," Eve said. "Every day. And we're not the only ones."

Hope tucked the note into her apron pocket, over her heart.

"Thank you," she whispered. "Both of you."

CHAPTER 28

The cottage was quiet when Hope returned that evening, save for the soft rustle of Ginger batting at a toy ball under the kitchen table. Tiger lay stretched out along the wide windowsill, watching the rising moon cast shadows across the verandah.

Hope flicked on the lamp beside her armchair. Its amber glow settled over the room, familiar and gentle. She toed off her shoes, set down her keys, and let the cottage's silence wrap around her like a shawl. It was the kind of quiet that made her shoulders drop. The ache of the day was giving way to stillness.

She made a cup of lemongrass and ginger tea, fingers curling around the warmth. Her body was exhausted, but her mind wouldn't relax. Something had stayed with her through the long, crowded hours of the fête. Something stronger than wariness, it felt more like resolve.

Beside her journal sat the note Eve had handed her. The folded edge was soft now, handled too many times to be crisp. Hope smoothed it open again, reading the words in the soft lamplight:

"Do not fear, for I am with you ..."

She breathed in the verse. A lifeline.

Tiger flicked his tail lazily. Ginger purred while pawing the rug then curled into a tight ball with a little sigh.

It had been a long day.

But she hadn't just stood. She had stayed.

She reached for her pen to write a few lines in her journal, when she heard a knock.

Three taps.

Measured. Calm. Unwelcome.

Hope's hand stilled above the page. Her eyes went to the clock.

9:18 p.m.

She rose slowly, placing the tea down. Ginger looked up, alert. Tiger sat up now, ears angled toward the door.

The knock came again. Slow, and deliberate.

Her chest tightened. She didn't need to look out the window.

She already knew who it was.

Hope opened the door a careful few inches, keeping her body behind it.

Mark stood just beyond the porch light's reach, wearing jeans and a button-up shirt that was too neat to have been worn all day. His hair was trimmed. His smile was practised.

"Evening, Hope," he said, voice low and warm, like he'd just come by to return something to a friend.

Her hand stayed on the doorframe. "It's late."

"I know. I wouldn't have come if it wasn't important."

"It's not appropriate to show up at my home at night. Uninvited."

He held up his hands. "I just needed a chance to speak with you privately. Without an audience. Without others interfering."

Hope didn't move. "You could have called."

"You wouldn't have answered."

He wasn't wrong. But she said nothing.

Mark tilted his head slightly, voice softening. "You look well. There's light in your eyes again. It's good to see."

Hope didn't reply.

"I've been praying about this," he continued, stepping forward slightly. "Us. About what God might want to restore. About what forgiveness really means."

Her spine straightened. "Forgiveness doesn't mean trust."

He blinked, caught off-guard. "It means reconciliation. Redemption. Second chances."

"No." Her voice was steady. "Forgiveness means letting go of the bitterness and resentment I feel towards you. It doesn't mean I will trust you again."

Mark's smile slipped, just briefly. He shifted his weight, the charm returning with effort.

"We made vows, Hope. Before God. And marriage … it's meant to reflect Christ's love. Enduring. Forgiving. Everlasting."

"I remember those vows," she said quietly. "I also remember you breaking every one of them."

His jaw twitched, just a flicker.

"I've changed," he said, softer now. "I'm not the man I was. The past few months … I've done a lot of soul-searching. I've been attending church again. Seeking God. Learning how I messed up. That has to count for something."

She stepped onto the porch, the door clicking shut behind her. Ruby wasn't far away, just over at the café if she needed help. But she didn't call out. Not yet. This was her moment to speak.

"If you've truly changed, then you know real repentance isn't about proving something to me. It's about owning what you did. The hurt you caused. The damage. The control. The fear."

Mark's expression darkened slightly. "I never laid a hand on you."

"You did lay a hand on me. But you were careful not to leave any marks or bruises. You constantly put me down. You destroyed things that you knew were precious to me. Blamed me for your anger and cruelty. You turned faith into a weapon and tried to crush me."

Silence stretched between them.

"I don't feel safe with you here," she added. "And I won't pretend I do to make you comfortable."

Mark tried a soft chuckle. "This isn't who you are. You've let people poison you against me."

Hope folded her arms. "No. I've remembered the person I was before."

His mask began to crack, with eyes narrowing slightly, and the corners of his mouth pulling tight.

Mark took a step closer. "I came here in good faith, Hope. You could at least hear me out properly."

"I've heard you," she said, not moving. "And I'm asking you to leave."

His tone dropped. "You're really going to throw away a decade of marriage because some new friends have turned you against me?"

"I left because you treated me like I was something to be controlled. Managed. Broken down. And because you were unfaithful."

"That's not true," he snapped. "I tried, Hope. I really did. You always made things harder than they had to be. You were so emotional. So sensitive. You turned every little disagreement into a crisis. Who could blame a guy in looking for support somewhere else."

"No," Hope said evenly. "You made every disagreement dangerous."

Mark's jaw clenched. "You're twisting things now."

"No, Mark. I'm finally telling the truth out loud."

A shadow passed across his face. The warmth was gone. "Well. No one's here to listen. You don't have anyone else left who'd want to share your life. You're worthless."

At that, Hope stepped back, opened the door and stepped back inside. "You need to go. Now."

But Mark didn't move. His voice was a sneer. "These people don't care about you. This little town? They'll drop you the moment they really get to know you."

From across the yard, there was a low growl.

Mark turned as Asha padded out of the darkness, hackles raised, a quiet warning vibrating from deep in her chest.

"Where'd this stray come from?" Mark snapped, as Asha stepped between him and the door. "Back off."

He raised his foot, as if to kick, and that's when Ruby stepped out of the shadows near the edge of the cottage.

"She's not the one who needs to back off," Ruby said, stepping forward, her voice like steel.

Mark spun around, startled. "What are you doing here?"

"I live here," Ruby said simply. "And I heard everything."

Hope exhaled shakily and stepped forward as Ruby walked across the verandah and stood beside her.

"If this is how you talk when you're claiming to be a changed man," Ruby added, "I'd hate to have seen you before."

Mark's mouth opened, then closed again.

"You're not welcome here," Ruby continued. "Not now. Not any night. Hope's not alone anymore."

Mark's eyes darted between them. Hope was unwavering, Ruby fierce, and Asha still growling softly nearby.

"You've made a mistake," he muttered, stepping back.

"No," Hope said. "Finally, I've stopped making them.

He hesitated a moment longer, then stalked toward his car, shoulders tense and stride tight with anger.

As the headlights flared and the engine started, Ruby reached for Hope's hand.

"I'm sleeping in the spare room," she said firmly. "And I'm not leaving again until I'm sure he's gone for good."

Hope didn't answer straight away. But when she did, her voice was low and grateful.

"Thank you."

Together, they stepped back inside with Asha and locked the door behind them.

***

The morning light crept in gently through the café's side window, casting long bars across the bench where Rowena was prepping the early trays of scones.

Ruby sat on a stool near the coffee machine, still in pyjamas and Hope's oversized hoodie. Her eyes were shadowed, her hair in a messy braid, but her voice was steady.

"He just showed up," she said, stirring sugar into her tea. "Late. Calm. Like it was normal to stand on someone's doorstep and be a bully."

Rowena stopped for a moment. "And Hope let him?"

"She was polite. Asked him to leave. He wouldn't. Started on about forgiveness and marriage vows." Ruby gave a sharp exhale. "She stood her ground though. Honestly? She was solid. She didn't raise her voice. Just named it all for what it was."

Rowena wiped her hands and turned fully toward her. "What happened next?"

Ruby looked down. "He got aggressive. Wasn't yelling, but you could feel his anger. He became nasty. Then Asha came over growling, and he tried to kick her."

Rowena's eyes widened. "He what?"

"I stepped in. Told him to leave. He did. But not nicely."

Silence hung in the room for a moment, broken only by the quiet hum of the fridge.

"Hope's not coming to church this morning," Ruby added. "She wrote a note and left it on the kitchen table saying that she couldn't go, not if he's going to be standing there, pretending."

"Fair enough," Rowena said grimly. "She shouldn't have to."

"She's gone for a drive. Took Asha. Just needed air, I think."

Rowena nodded slowly. "And you?"

"I'm going," Ruby said firmly. "To church. So, people know what actually happened. You don't get to behave like that and then keep smiling in the front pew."

Rowena gave a small, proud smile. "I'll come with you."

"Really?"

"Absolutely. I've seen enough charmers in my day. And I believe Hope."

Ruby picked up her tea. "Thanks. I know this might get messy."

Rowena's eyes narrowed. "Good. Sometimes truth is."

***

Hope had left the cottage earlier that morning, after writing a note for Ruby and locking the door.

She needed quiet. Space. Somewhere away from questions and watching eyes.

With Asha in the passenger seat, head lolling out the window, she turned the car toward mountains. She didn't know yet what she would pray. Only that she needed to remember who she was, and whose she was.

As the road wound higher into the Highlands, Hope whispered Eve's verse again under her breath.

I will strengthen and help you ...
And she believed it.
Even now.

***

Back at the café, Ruby pulled on her boots and glanced at the clock. The church bell hadn't started ringing yet, but it would. Soon.

Rowena handed her a travel mug of tea. "Let's go."

CHAPTER 29

The church service had ended with a chorus of "Amazing Grace" and the murmur of fellowship. Mark stood near the back pews, relaxed, smiling, effortlessly slipping into easy conversation with Steve and Mike. He chuckled at something Steve said, clapped him on the back, and made a warm comment about the message.

He looked like he belonged.

After everyone had wandered over to the hall, Ruby watched from a quiet corner by the doorway, her arms folded across her chest, Rowena standing next to her. She scanned the room until she spotted Eve and Pastor Tom standing near the kitchen servery, sipping tea. Gathering her courage, Ruby whispered to Rowena, and they crossed the room.

"Eve? Pastor Tom?" Her voice was quiet but steady.

They turned to her.

"I need to talk to you about something that happened last night. With Mark."

Eve's eyes sharpened. Tom lowered his mug and gave a single nod.

"Of course," he said. "Let's move to a quieter place back in the church."

When Tom, Eve and Rowena were all seated, Ruby took a deep breath and recounted what had happened at the cottage, with the confrontation, Mark's tone, and the undercurrents of intimidation. She was careful, calm, not dramatic. Her words carried weight because of their honest simplicity.

Tom listened without interrupting. When she finished, he looked out the doors towards the church hall, where Mark was now chatting with a couple near the entrance.

"Thank you," he said quietly. "You did the right thing. Both last night and talking to me now."

He walked over to Dave Sullivan, who was just leaving the vestry after counting the offertory. Dave was tall, broad-shouldered, in jeans and a checked shirt. Though technically off-duty this morning, the local police officer still carried that unmistakable air of steadiness about him. He was also one of the church elders, and someone Tom trusted implicitly.

Tom murmured a few words to him, and Dave gave a small nod.

Now outside, Tom approached Mark with his usual pastoral warmth. "Mark, I wonder if you'd have a few minutes to chat in the rectory. Just a quick catch-up. Dave is going to join us."

Mark, not correcting Tom on his recent preference for *Jamie*, smiled broadly. "Of course, Pastor. I've been hoping for a chance to talk."

***

The room was sunlit and simple. A Bible sat open on the coffee table. Tom gestured to the armchairs.

"Thanks for making time," he began. "I wanted to check in. It's clear you've been making connections around the church. What brings you back again to Wombat Valley this weekend, Mark?"

Mark settled back, adopting an earnest tone. "I've changed, Tom. God's been working on me. I love Hope. I came back to rebuild, to ask for a second chance. Marriage is sacred, and I want to honour that. I know we had struggles, but with God, there's always redemption."

Tom nodded slowly. "Redemption is a beautiful thing. But it always begins with truth."

Mark blinked. "Absolutely."

"Then let's talk about what that truth really is," Tom said calmly. "Hope's shared with us the nature of your past relationship. Your controlling behaviour, her belongings you smashed, the shouting. And the emotional manipulation. She mentioned you were seeing someone else, even while you were still married and living together."

Mark scoffed gently, the smile slipping just a little. "You have to understand, Hope was grieving her mother. She wasn't herself. She would twist things, make them sound worse than they were. She always tended to … well, catastrophise."

Tom leaned forward slightly.

"Grief affects perception. Yes.

But it doesn't smash belongings.

It doesn't instil fear.

And it doesn't use coercive control … like the way you spoke to Hope in front of Ruby at the cottage last night."

Mark's tone sharpened. "Ruby's a teenager. Impressionable. She misunderstood." He hesitated. "I was just trying to reach out to reconnect with Hope."

Dave hadn't spoken yet, but his presence was steady beside the door.

Tom met Mark's gaze. "Let me ask you something directly. What work have you actually done to confront the shame beneath your need for control? Or the insecurity that might be driving your need to intimidate others?"

Mark's eyes narrowed, not in confusion, but in defiance. "I don't think that's a fair question."

Tom's voice remained gentle but firm. "I think it's an essential one."

Mark shifted in his seat. "I've told you … I've changed. God's forgiven me."

Tom nodded slowly. "God's forgiveness is real, but it doesn't entitle anyone to step back into a relationship they broke. Forgiveness is God's gift. But trust is earned. Reconciliation requires safety and truth. Repentance shows itself through change, not just in words, but in consistent, demonstrated actions over time."

He opened the Bible on the table, flipping to a marked page. "This might sound harsh, but it's Scripture we can't ignore. The Apostle Paul speaks clearly: '*Do not associate with anyone who claims to be a brother or sister but is sexually immoral or greedy, or is an idolater, slanderer, drunkard or swindler. Do not even eat with such people*' (1 Corinthians 5:11)."

Mark stiffened.

Tom continued, turning more pages. "And again, '*Keep away from every believer who is idle and disruptive and does not live according to the teaching you received from us*' (2 Thessalonians 3:6)."

He looked up. "Mark, you've come here claiming faith. But you've lied about Hope. Slandered her. Tried to re-enter her life without real accountability."

Mark stood abruptly. "You're judging me."

"I'm shepherding this church," Tom said calmly. "And my duty is to protect the vulnerable, not entertain deception."

The room fell still. Sunlight spilled through the window, but the warmth no longer touched Mark's expression.

Tom's voice remained steady. "You've said you've changed. But what I see, Mark, is a pattern. A need to control the narrative. To control people.

You've misrepresented the past. You have approached Hope under false pretences and frightened a young woman outside her own home."

Mark bristled, his eyes hardening.

"That girl is making things up. She doesn't know what she saw."

"I believe she does," Tom said, not blinking. "And I believe Hope. She has been honest, humble, and willing to walk in the light. What I'm hearing from you sounds like manipulation, not repentance."

Mark's tone turned cold.

"I didn't come here to be interrogated. I came to reconcile with my wife and connect with this church."

Tom met his gaze.

"You came here to reclaim control.

That's not reconciliation.

And it's not welcome."

Mark's posture stiffened, and for a flicker of a moment, the charm drained away. What remained was cold. Calculating.

"You think you can stand in judgment over me?" Mark spat. "You don't even know me."

Dave stepped forward. "We know enough."

Mark's eyes swung to him.

"Who even are you? Tom's muscle?"

Dave's voice was quiet, but it carried the weight of someone used to setting boundaries that mattered. "I'm Dave Sullivan. One of the church elders, and also a police officer. I've seen your type before, Mark. And I'm telling you clearly, your behaviour has crossed a line."

Mark's lips curled into a sneer, but something had shifted behind his eyes. It was calculation giving way to fury.

He stood and stepped closer, fists tight at his sides.

"You think you can keep me away? I'll talk to people. The town knows me. They'll hear my side—"

Tom raised a hand gently.

"No, Mark. They've already heard enough. Your story doesn't hold under the weight of truth. And this church, this community, is choosing truth. We will not allow unsafe behaviour. Not from anyone. You are not welcome here today, or any day, until you can demonstrate true repentance. Over time. With accountability."

Mark's voice dropped, venomous. "You'll see who people really believe."

Something in him shifted. Gone was the charm. What stood before them now was the cold face of control, unmasked and unrepentant.

Dave stepped closer. "Leave. Now."

Mark took a long moment, breathing hard, his face twitching with fury. But the confrontation was lost. The old tricks had failed.

He turned sharply and stormed out with a muttered curse, his mask now broken. The man underneath exposed.

The door slammed behind him.

Tom sat back down, exhaling. There was no triumph for him. Only grief for the damage done. His prayer was that one day truth might take root in even the hardest of hearts.

"Didn't expect him to crack that fast," Dave said.

"He's used to people believing the performance," Tom replied. "When that doesn't work, he is quick to anger."

They sat in silence for a moment. The quiet was full of weight, but also peace.

Tom looked at Dave. "Thanks for being here."

Dave gave a short nod. "This time, the shepherd had a staff. And backup."

Tom smiled faintly. "That's what the flock deserves."

CHAPTER 30

Tom had asked them to meet after lunch.

They gathered in the room at the back of the church's hall. The one with the faded carpet, a battered kettle, and mismatched chairs around a heavy old timber table. There was nothing ornate or sacred in here, but just the kind of quiet that invited honesty.

Joe came in, nodding to the others. Dave was already there, arms folded. Steve and Mike arrived next, looking uncertain, like they weren't sure what this was going to be about.

Tom didn't rush them. He poured mugs of tea, passed them around, then sat down last.

"Thanks for coming," he said simply. "This isn't a meeting. There's no agenda. Just something we need to talk about, man to man. Brother to brother."

They nodded, subdued.

"I want to tell you plainly what happened this morning," Tom continued. "Mark came to church again today. Smiling. Shaking hands. Playing the part. Ruby told Eve and I about what happened at Hope's cottage last night, how he turned up, and how he spoke to her. It matched the same pattern Hope described."

He paused, letting the silence settle.

"I asked Mark to come to the rectory after the service. Dave was with me. Mark started out saying that he'd changed, that he wanted to rebuild his marriage. But when I pressed him on his behaviour, on his patterns, and the damage he's done, the mask slipped. He got angry. Defensive. Wouldn't take responsibility. Dave stepped in. Told him who he was. Mark left, furious. We told him clearly: he's not welcome back here unless he shows real repentance and change. Not words, actions."

A long silence followed.

Mike frowned. "I mean … people change, right? I thought maybe he was trying."

Dave spoke quietly. "I've seen men like that before. In uniform, out of uniform. They know how to perform. How to say all the right things … until they're told no."

Steve let out a breath. "I didn't see it," he admitted. "I just thought … he seemed so genuine. He asked me to pray for him last week. I thought I was helping."

Tom gave a small nod. "That's not your fault. That's what abusers who want to control others often rely on, people who want to believe the best about them."

Joe looked down at his mug. "If people at their last church had looked more closely, maybe Hope wouldn't have had to walk through it alone."

Tom nodded, his voice low. "Maybe not. But we can choose what kind of men we'll be. Here, in this church."

He looked each man in the eye.

"Brothers, we've been called to more than polite Sunday fellowship. We've been asked by God to reflect His heart, His justice, His protection, and His wisdom. That means having the courage to see through false appearances. Jesus warned us about wolves in sheep's clothing. To look out for those who seem godly on the outside but are full of self and pride."

He turned his Bible on the table and opened it gently.

"*Whoever covers an offense seeks love, but he who repeats a matter separates close friends*' (Proverbs 17:9)."

He glanced up. "Sin separates. Us from God, and from one another. And it's not godly to pretend everything's fine when there's no repentance."

He turned to another page.

"*Do not be misled: Bad company corrupts good character*'. (1 Corinthians 15:33). And again, '*Do not associate with anyone who claims to be a brother but is a slanderer ... or a swindler ...*' (1 Corinthians 5:11)."

Tom looked at them.

"God doesn't ask us to maintain fellowship with those who wound others without remorse. Extending grace doesn't mean enabling sin or turning a blind eye. That's not grace. That's denial."

The room stayed quiet. No one interrupted.

Tom's tone softened. "It's hard to admit we've been taken in. Harder still to admit we didn't act when we should have. Sometimes we cling to a person's story because the alternative is admitting we were wrong. But pride doesn't protect people, it only protects our egos. And we weren't called to that."

Joe looked up slowly. "So, what do we do now?"

Tom's voice was steady. "We live differently. We stay alert. We listen. We can believe women when they speak. We don't leave them to carry it alone. We make sure that this church, and this town, becomes the kind of place where truth and protection aren't optional."

He leaned back slightly, eyes kind but firm.

"It's not too late to be the kind of men God calls us to be. The kind who protect others. Who pursue truth."

Steve glanced at Tom, his face tense. "But how do we know where that line is? I mean every guy raises his voice sometimes. We're not all manipulators."

Tom looked at him steadily. "No, we're not. But we are responsible for how we use our voices. Our strength. And if someone says they were afraid, or that behaviours make them feel unsafe, we have to ask why. Not defend people first."

Steve looked away, jaw tight.

Dave looked around the table. "It's not just about what happened with Mark. It's about what kind of community we're building. What kind of men we're encouraging. I've got two daughters. And I want them growing up in a place where men understand that God didn't give us strength to control and intimidate, but to carry carefully. To protect. Not exploit."

Steve blinked, and something shifted in his posture. His hand tightened slightly around his mug. He thought of Ava, his daughter, seven years old. She was fierce and bright and watching everything.

No one rushed to respond. But something shifted around that table. Not loud. Not dramatic. But real.

A quiet kind of resolve.

Steve swallowed and nodded. "I want to be that kind of man."

Joe looked down at his hands, then up at Tom.

"And I think Hope deserves to know she's not alone anymore."

The others nodded. No one spoke for a moment.

Then Steve said, quieter now, "We've got work to do."

But in his eyes was something new. Not defiance, and not certainty. Recognition. And the beginning of discomfort.

Tom looked around the room. "That's where it starts."

***

Hope had driven out before dawn, the roads still cloaked in morning mist. She didn't have a destination in mind, only the need to go. She needed to put distance between herself and the fear that had returned with a knock on her door and a voice she thought she'd never hear again.

Asha rode in the back seat, quiet and alert, occasionally resting her chin on Hope's shoulder when the car stopped near a lookout or slowed over a creek crossing. Hope had prayed in fragments, both for help and to ask God questions that had no shape.

By late afternoon, she'd returned to the cottage, weary but steadier. She'd watered the garden, fed the cats, and brewed herself a mug of chamomile tea. Ruby and Rowena were still at the café tidying up after the lunch crowd they'd served after church.

The phone rang just as Hope had settled on the couch, Tiger and Ginger curled up at her feet.

It was Tom.

"Hope," he said gently, "I wanted to check in. And I was wondering if Eve and I could drop by for a few minutes. Nothing heavy, just a visit to let you know about what happened this morning after church."

Something in his voice gave her pause.

"Yes," she said, quietly. "That would be okay."

Twenty minutes later, she heard the car pull up. Asha was outside on the verandah wagging her tail at the familiar visitors. Hope opened the door before they knocked.

Tom stood with Eve, both of them holding a kind of reverent calm, like they knew this wasn't just a social call.

"Come in," Hope said.

They stepped inside, the warmth of the little cottage wrapping around them. Eve set down a small plate of chocolate brownies she'd baked.

They sat in the loungeroom, and Tom didn't waste time.

"We confronted Mark this morning," he said.

Hope blinked. "You ... what?"

"I spoke with Ruby after the service," he continued. "She told us what happened last night. I invited Mark to the rectory to speak privately. Dave was there too."

Hope stared at him. "Did you believe Ruby? About what happened?"

Tom met her gaze with a gentleness that cut straight through.

"Yes. We did."

She didn't speak. Her fingers gripped the rim of her mug. Tom went on, steady and clear letting her know about how Mark had tried to explain things away, how the story didn't add up, how the truth became undeniable. He told her what he'd said, word for word, that Mark was not welcome back unless there was true repentance. That her safety mattered.

Hope didn't cry. She just blinked, trying to process what she'd heard.

Eve reached out gently and took her hand. "You're not alone anymore," she said softly.

Hope didn't speak. Her nails pressed into the ceramic mug. The tea had gone cold, but she held it like a tether to something real. Tom's words saying, 'we believed you, he's not welcome, you are safe', swirled around her like a language she used to know but hadn't heard in years.

She wasn't crying. She wasn't even breathing properly. Just sitting there, eyes wide, as if trying to take in air and truth at the same time.

Eve saw it first. The shock. The stiffness in Hope's shoulders, the blank stillness behind her eyes.

Tom softened his voice. "Hope ... I know this might be a lot to take in all at once."

Hope blinked slowly, as though surfacing from underwater.

"You don't have to say anything right now," Eve added gently. "There's no pressure to process this straight away. We just wanted you to know the truth, and to reassure you that you're not alone anymore."

Tom nodded. "We're both here in town to support you, and we'll keep being there for you."

Hope managed a small nod. Her lips parted slightly, like she wanted to say something, but she closed them again and looked down at her hands.

Eve reached out gently and squeezed her fingers.

After a few more minutes of quiet presence, with no advice, no fixing, only kindness, they rose to leave.

Tom put a hand lightly on Hope's shoulder. "Call if you need anything."

Hope didn't trust her voice, but she quietly whispered, "Thank you."

The door clicked softly shut behind them.

Only then did she exhale.

She sat unmoving for a long while, the quiet of the cottage pressing in gently around her like a blanket. The room hadn't changed. But she had. Just a little. Enough to know that she didn't need to be alone anymore. With her hands still trembling slightly, she picked up the phone and dialled.

"Hey," she said, her voice a low rasp. "Joe ... are you free? I think I just ... need a friend to talk to for a while."

***

The sun had dipped low behind the hills by the time Joe pulled into the drive. The cool of the afternoon had set in quickly, a blue-edged hush that came over Wombat Valley in the early evening. Her porch light was on.

Hope opened the front door before he reached the steps. She had changed into a warm soft jumper, with faded blue jeans. Her eyes were tired but clearer than before.

199

"Thanks for coming," she said quietly.

"No problem," Joe replied.

Inside, Ruby was already tidying up the tea things in the kitchen, having come back from the café not long after Tom and Eve had left. Asha was stretched out in her usual spot, chin on paws, thumping her tail gently when Joe entered.

They sat in the lounge area, with Ruby perched on a kitchen stool near Hope, casually present, and quietly supportive. The kettle was warm again, and the air smelled faintly of chamomile.

"I heard from Tom what happened this morning," Joe said, settling onto the couch opposite. "He told me about the confrontation. And he asked a few of us men to meet after lunch, just Dave, Steve, Mike … and me."

Hope looked up at that. Uncertainty, flickering behind her eyes.

Joe went on. "Tom didn't just confront Mark. He challenged us too, as brothers. He told us that Mark wasn't safe. That he's shown no signs of repentance. That charm can be a mask, and that silence is a form of complicity. He also said that as men of faith we can't just sit by and hope things sort themselves out. Our silence has consequences."

Hope didn't say anything, but her posture softened slightly. The tension in her shoulders eased just enough to notice.

Joe offered a faint smile. "He was clear. Really clear. That you're part of this church family now. That you deserve our trust. Our respect. That we've got a role to play, and that men in our church have got some growing to do."

Hope looked down at her hands, the silence stretching. Her fingers traced the rim of her mug again, then stopped.

"Why did he do this for me?"

Joe leaned forward a little, elbows on knees.

"Because you matter, Hope. Because the truth matters. And because God hasn't forgotten you, not for one moment."

Her lips trembled. She set her mug down quickly, both hands coming to cover her mouth. Her breath hitched, and then the tears came.

They were just the slow, shaking weep of someone who'd held her breath for too long.

Ruby reached over and laid a hand gently on her back. She didn't speak, but her eyes shimmered. Something in her sensed the weight of this moment. How earth-shattering it was for Hope to not be met with suspicion by a church community, but with belief. With trust. Protection. It felt like ... a turning point. The beginning of healing.

Joe stayed where he was, present but steady.

"You're safe," Ruby whispered. "You're safe now."

Hope leaned into the couch cushions, head bowed, shoulders quivering. She didn't fight the tears this time.

She let them fall.

When the storm passed, she wiped at her cheeks, eyes puffy and dazed. "I didn't know what it would feel like," she murmured. "To be believed."

Joe gave her a quiet nod, then asked, "would you like me to pray with you?"

She nodded, her voice too fragile for words.

Joe prayed. He spoke slow, steady words of thanks, protection, and healing. He asked for peace, for the restoration of trust, for the warmth of God's presence to fill the quiet places of Hope's heart.

When he finished, he gave her a long, searching look. It wasn't heavy with pity, but full of respect.

"You don't have to carry this alone anymore."

Hope nodded, another tear tracing down her cheek. "Thank you," she whispered.

Joe stood, giving Ruby a gentle look, then let himself out, leaving the door unlocked.

Hope sat for a while longer.

Ruby gently draped a blanket over Hope's shoulders, then leaned in and wrapped her arms around her.

No words. Just warmth.

And the beginning of peace.

CHAPTER 31

The next morning was still. The café was closed for its usual Monday rest day, and the town felt hushed beneath a soft mist that clung to the gums and curled above the surface of the Wombat River.

Hope had woken before sunrise. Her body was rested, but her spirit felt restless, not with anxiety, but with an internal stirring. It felt like something that had been dormant was now slowly waking up.

She'd sat at the kitchen table for a long time with her Bible open, untouched for a week. It had fallen open to the Gospel of John. She hadn't planned to read that far, but her eyes had been drawn to a heading near the end: Jesus Prays for All Believers.

She read slowly, as if tasting something unfamiliar:

"My prayer is not for them alone. I pray also for those who will believe in me through their message, that all of them may be one, Father, just as you are in me and I am in you ..."

Her finger lingered on the words.

"... Then the world will know that you sent me and have loved them even as you have loved me."

Hope stared at the page, the verses blurring for a moment. Then her eyes focused on the line:

"... that all of them may be one."

She'd read that passage before. Years ago. Back when she thought God was only interested in the faithful and whole, not the fractured. But this morning, the words felt alive, not as an ideal, but as something she had actually glimpsed.

Unity in God's family. Love. Real protection.

She had seen it yesterday: in Tom's courage, in Eve's tenderness, in Joe's steady presence, and in Ruby's quiet faithfulness.

For the first time in a very long time, she believed that Jesus' prayer was possible.

She closed the Bible slowly, held it against her chest, and breathed in deep.

***

By mid-morning, she found herself walking down the track to the river, Asha trotting at her side.

The Wombat River shimmered ahead, the sun catching on the water like a scattering of silver threads. The banks were quiet, undisturbed. She stepped out onto the low rock ledge near the water's edge and stood for a long time, looking out.

"I didn't think I'd ever come back," she whispered.

Asha sat beside her, leaning gently against her knee.

Hope looked up at the sky, then back at the water. "But You never stopped seeing me. You never stopped calling me, did You?"

Her voice caught, trembling, but the tears held back.

"I walked away. I carried so much anger. Not just at Mark … but at You. For not stopping it. For not protecting me back then. For letting people turn away."

She exhaled shakily.

"I thought You'd abandoned me … but now I see it wasn't You. It was people, broken, proud, and confused people. But You've shown me something different now, through others."

She stepped closer to the water's edge, crouched, and let her fingers trail into the current.

"I want to be part of Your family again.

Not just the church family.

I want to belong to You."

The tears came then, quiet and cleansing.

"I repent," she whispered. "For walking away. For letting bitterness bury me. For my anger towards you. I want to be washed clean. I want to come home."

The river moved around her fingers, gentle and unhurried. A sign. A grace.

***

The following Sunday was the first weekend in winter. It was the kind of morning where the sun breaks through the chill just enough to stir something in the soul. Church had ended not long before, and some of the congregation had followed one another in a convoy of cars and utes out to the riverbank at the western edge of Edith and Rob's property.

Hope now stood at the water's edge, a borrowed wetsuit from the local kayak adventure company zipped up awkwardly over a layer of thermals. The sun shimmered off the Wombat River as it flowed past, clear and cold, curling around mossy rocks and the knees of ancient gums. It should have been freezing, but warmth pulsed in her chest like firelight.

Tom stood to one side, already ankle-deep in the river, chest-high fishing waders on, sleeves rolled up, a joyful steadiness about him. Beside him was his wife Eve, also suited up, a steady presence who had prayed with Hope many times now, had opened the Bible to share God's words, and sat with her in silence when she couldn't speak. Her presence in the river felt like a quiet blessing, strong, motherly, and deeply faithful.

On the banks, a small crowd had gathered to watch Hope's baptism. Ruby was easy to spot, wrapped in a thick wool coat, her hands resting on the gentle curve of her belly, a radiant glow on her face that went beyond pregnancy. Craig stood nearby her, though his attention drifted often to where Nova stood just a few steps away. Nova's daughter Lily clung gently to her mother's hand, wide-eyed and curious, her other hand gripping the battered sketchpad she often carried.

Rowena stood nearby, arms folded across her chest, her expression unsure, but attentive. She hadn't said much about the whole thing, just asked if she could come over the coffee machine that morning. "I'm not completely sold on the idea of faith, but … I'm interested. Watching your Pastor Tom be willing to hear the truth about Mark, and defend you, was a powerful witness."

Joe stood quietly apart, as he often did in crowds, a warm smile on his face, his eyes steady on Hope. She met his gaze, and the world seemed to still for a moment. Then she turned toward Tom and Eve, stepping carefully into the water.

She gasped as the cold bit at her skin, but neither she nor Eve flinched. Eve's hand wrapped around hers as they moved deeper. Tom spoke softly, the words steady and sure, meant not just for her ears but for her soul.

"Hope, today you come not just to water, but to life. Do you believe Jesus is the Son of God, who brings new life?"

Hope nodded, a tremble in her lips that had nothing to do with the cold. "I do."

"Is it your desire to follow Him, as your Lord and Saviour?"

"It is."

Tom's voice was gentler now. "Then I baptise you in the name of the Father, the Son, and the Holy Spirit."

The sky, wide and blue above her, looked like a dome as she sank beneath the surface.

For a moment, silence. The weightless hush of water.

And then … light. Breath. Air. The roaring sound of joy as she rose up, sputtering and laughing through her tears.

On the riverbank, someone clapped.

Lily's voice piped up, clear and small. "She looks shiny!"

Hope laughed again, pushing wet hair from her face. Eve wrapped an arm around her shoulders.

She was shaking, not just from the cold, but from something deeper.

A cleansing.

A release.

Her spirit was singing.

She was not who she had been.

A towel was wrapped around Hope's shoulders before she even reached the bank. She wasn't sure whose hands had done it. There were too many arms folding her into hugs, laughter, tears, and warm woollen sleeves against damp skin.

"Welcome home, love," Edith whispered, her voice thick with tears. "God had not forgotten you."

Ruby hugged her gently but tight, one hand resting protectively on her belly. "You did it," she grinned. "I look up to you so much and I'm so thankful that that we are both finding our way to faith." Craig offered an awkward but sincere pat on the shoulder, while Lily presented her with a freshly drawn picture, with stick figures in the river under a blazing yellow sun. "That's you, and that's God," Lily explained, pointing. "He's the big smile in the sky."

Rowena hovered nearby, hands in her pockets, her usual harsh practical voice softened. "That was ... something," she said, blinking quickly. "Might not understand it, but it looked like it mattered."

Hope smiled. "It did. More than I can say."

Then Nova stepped forward, quiet and steady. She didn't say anything at first. Just opened her arms.

Hope walked into them, the towel still clutched around her and held on tight. For a long moment, neither of them spoke.

It was Nova who had offered her the first real invitation back to church, not to fix anything, not to explain herself, but just to come. One nervous Sunday, sitting beside Nova in the back pew, Hope had cried quietly through every song. Nova hadn't tried to convince her or pried about her church past. She simply opened the door for Hope to walk through.

Now, as the breeze stirred the trees above them, Nova pulled back slightly, hands still on Hope's arms. Her eyes glistened.

"I knew you were meant to find your way back to faith," she said softly. "Even when I wasn't sure I was. You gave me courage, by providing a safe refuge."

Hope felt a lump rise in her throat. "I thought if you can find your way to trust God after so recently being in danger, I certainly could try too. So, thank you."

Nova shrugged lightly, brushing a strand of hair from her face. "God's the one who was chasing you down. But I'm glad I got to be part of the nudge."

They both laughed, quiet and teary.

A soft voice spoke behind them.

"It was like watching someone walk through fire and come out with no smoke on their skin."

They turned to see Hanna, her coat buttoned to the neck, cheeks pink from the cold. She held a thermos of tea she'd brought to share and looked at Hope like someone witnessing a miracle up close.

"I've only seen baptism once before," she continued, stepping closer. "In Poland, when I was a girl. It was quiet, ritualistic. But this ... looked like freedom."

Hope blinked, moved by her honesty.

Hanna glanced toward the river, then back to Hope. "You said once that you weren't sure if God saw you. But today ..." She gestured toward the sky. "I think heaven was watching."

Hope smiled, the tears returning.

Hanna reached out and touched the towel wrapped around Hope's shoulders lightly, reverently. "I don't know everything about faith yet. But I do know this. Whatever you left in that water ... it's gone. And what you came out with, it's fresh and new."

For a moment, none of them spoke.

Then Hanna gave a quick nod, her voice softening. "I'm very proud to know you."

Hope reached for her hand, squeezing it. "I'm glad you were here."

Hanna smiled. "I wouldn't have missed it for anything."

A few steps behind her, her husband Marcel gave a small wave. He stood beside a folding picnic chair where Hanna had laid a spare blanket and a basket of pastries she'd brought "just in case anyone needed carbs after a holy moment."

He wore a thick navy coat and a polite smile, his breath misting in the cold. Hope had only met him a couple of times, in the florist shop mostly, but he always struck her as kind. Observant. Quiet in the way of someone who thought deeply but spoke rarely.

Hanna turned and beckoned him forward. "Come. You can congratulate her too."

He stepped closer, a little unsure, then extended his hand.

"That was …" He paused, searching for the right word. "Powerful."

Hope shook his hand, surprised by the earnestness in his voice. "Thank you. I wasn't sure I could go through with it."

"Well, you did," Marcel said, then added with a wry smile, "and without fainting in the river from the cold, which is more than I could've managed."

Hanna elbowed him lightly. "He doesn't like cold water. Or early mornings. Or public expressions of anything."

"Especially all three together," Marcel admitted.

They laughed, and Hope felt the warmth of it reach somewhere deeper than skin.

Hanna looked at her husband, then back to Hope. "Marcel says he's not religious. But today I think even he was misty-eyed."

"I was not," Marcel objected, wiping the corner of one eye discreetly. "That was just the wind."

Hope grinned observing the still air. "Well, I'm glad you were both here. Truly."

Hanna nodded, linking her arm through Marcel's. "You're part of the bouquet now," she said with a wink. "All of us are. Different flowers, same garden."

As they moved away, Hope looked around—at Eve and Tom chatting nearby, at the cluster of friends, and at Joe standing down near the water, hands still in his jacket pockets, looking out with an expression of awe.

***

Most of the group had begun to drift back toward the parked cars, drawn by the promise of hot soup, fresh bread, and Edith's famous passionfruit slice waiting back at the café. Laughter and the murmur of happy conversation faded into the distance, leaving the riverbank momentarily quiet.

Hope stepped down the grassy slope, towel still wrapped around her shoulders. Joe was now sitting alone at the water's edge, elbows on his knees, eyes closed. The sunlight caught the side of his face. She saw his expression was calm, but his features were softened in an expression she couldn't read.

She hesitated, then walked a little closer. "Hey," she said quietly. "Are you okay?"

Joe opened his eyes slowly and looked up at her. He nodded, and for a moment didn't speak, just gave her that open, steady look she'd come to know. The one that didn't ask anything of her, didn't rush to fill silence.

Then he stood, brushing his hands on his jeans, his voice low and a little rough.

"I'm okay. Just … full." He gave a half-laugh. "In the best way."

She tilted her head. "Full?"

Joe glanced out at the river, where the ripples still moved gently over the rocks, reflecting the bright winter sky. "I've seen people lose their faith, Hope. Seen them get crushed by life, or grief, or shame … and never come back. And I've prayed for a lot of them. But watching you come up out of that water …" He stopped, eyes shining. "I don't think I've ever seen anything more beautiful."

Hope looked away, emotion tightening her throat. The water still dripped from her hair, sliding down her cheek. She wiped it away with the edge of the towel.

Joe continued, voice quieter now. "God never stops reaching, even when we're running. And when He brings someone home, it's not just a return.

It's a restoration. You're not the same as you were before. You're stronger. You're … more precious."

She looked at him then, and for a moment they simply stood there, river behind them, voices of their friends carrying faintly on the breeze.

Hope smiled, a tear slipping down her cheek. "Thank you. For your prayers. For not trying to rush me or fix me. For just being there."

Joe offered a small, warm smile. "That's how God's grace works, right? It finds us where we are. And then it walks with us."

He didn't try to hug her or hold her hand. He just stood with her. And in that silence, Hope felt the deep peace of being fully seen and not needing to be anything but what she already was: restored, and rising.

A voice called from the paddock. Edith, letting them know the cars were heading off. Joe nodded toward the slope. "Better not keep them waiting. You've got a piece of passionfruit slice with your name on it."

Hope laughed. "Now that is motivation."

And together, they walked back up the bank, the river sparkling behind them, lunch and laughter ahead.

CHAPTER 32

The café was closed, but the smell of freshly ground coffee still lingered in the air. Hope sat at the corner table near the front window, a steaming mug cradled between her hands. The winter sun filtered through the glass, warming the space in slow, golden rays.

A stack of unopened mail lay beside her, most of it bills and advertising. But one envelope, thick and official-looking, bore the letterhead of her solicitor. She opened it slowly, her heart thudding.

The signed divorce papers sat neatly inside, Mark's familiar signature scrawled in the last space.

It was done.

She had only dared to hope it would be this straightforward. Months ago, she'd sent the documents off with a prayer and quiet resolve. There was no legal battle, no contest over assets, and no more emotional entanglement. She'd let go of any claim to the house they once shared, anything that might give Mark one more excuse to stay in control. With her parents' inheritance, she didn't need it. All she'd wanted was freedom.

Now, it was in her hands.

There was no dramatic rush of relief, no burst of elation. Just a quiet, deep breath, and the strange, steady feeling of something closing cleanly. A chapter finished.

The little brass bell over the front door jingled.

She looked up to see Joe step inside, cheeks flushed from the cold, a woollen beanie pulled low over his ears.

"I thought you were taking the day off," he said, glancing at the mug in her hands and the paperwork surrounding her.

"I am." She smiled. "Almost. Just needed a quiet spot and something warm."

He nodded and crossed to the counter, making himself a coffee without needing to ask. Then he came over and took the seat opposite her, eyeing the papers on the table.

"Everything alright?"

Hope nodded, then pushed the unfolded pages toward him. "It's done. The divorce came through."

Joe glanced at the papers, then back at her, his expression unreadable for a moment.

"How do you feel?"

She looked out the window. "Lighter. Like something I've been dragging behind me just let go. No bitterness. No fear. Just peace."

He let out a quiet breath. "That's a gift."

She nodded. "It really is."

A moment later, Ruby emerged from the back, cheeks glowing. "You two sunbaking out here?" she teased. "I came in here to make a hot chocolate, and the baby just kicked again. It's the third time this morning. Little one's having a party in there."

Hope stood to hug her, laughing. "That's exciting! Was it really the first time you felt it yesterday?"

"Yep. Guess my baby wanted to celebrate your baptism too."

Joe smiled. "It has good taste, this baby."

As Ruby sipped her drink and leaned on the counter, talk turned to what lay ahead. They spoke of where she might live when the baby arrived, and how the flat behind the rectory was one option. Nova was thinking about moving herself and Lily into a place of their own.

There was so much yet to be worked out, but somehow none of it felt heavy.

Then Joe cleared his throat and looked toward Hope.

"Actually … I was wondering if you'd come for a drive. I want to show you something."

***

The gravel road wound through patchy farmland, golden grass catching the low winter light as Joe's ute drove along. Hope sat in the passenger seat, still feeling the warmth of the café and the quiet joy of the day before. She watched the hills roll past, all familiar now. A landscape that was home.

"Did you always know you wanted to live in a country town?" she asked.

Joe smiled faintly, eyes on the road. "I think I knew I eventually wanted space. Not just land, but room to grow something new. If it's God's will for me, maybe even a family one day."

He turned off onto a narrower track, slightly overgrown. A weathered wooden gate stood ahead, half-hanging on its hinges. Joe pulled up and opened it by hand. Then he drove through, stopping beside a small hill that overlooked a broad paddock bordered by gum trees and the river.

"This is it. I've had my offer accepted," he said simply.

Hope climbed out. The air was cold and sharp, the silence almost complete except for the distant caw of cockatoos. The old farmhouse stood back against the tree line on the hill. It was weatherboard, with peeling paint and a verandah railing that sagged. But it had good bones. The kind of house that could build and hold stories.

Joe walked a few steps ahead, then turned to face her. "It needs a lot of work," he said. "But I've started clearing it out. Craig's said he would help with the renos. I'm taking it one step at a time."

As they turned toward the house, a sharp bark rang out from the other side of the orchard.

Hope startled slightly, but Joe just grinned.

"That'll be Rusty," he said. "Not mine. Bounty is enough for me to keep an eye on. She belongs to the neighbours."

A red kelpie tore through the long grass, tail high, ears alert. She skidded to a halt in front of Joe, tongue lolling, then trotted up to Hope and leaned heavily against her legs as if she belonged there.

"She's friendly," Hope said, laughing as she reached down to rub behind the dog's ears.

"Too friendly. Doesn't respect fences yet," Joe said, ruffling her fur. "Her owner just moved in next door with his grandfather. They're in the old Walker place. It's a bit run-down, but he's keen to fix it up. Name's Jesse. Young bloke. Bit rough around the edges, but I reckon he's got good in him."

A young man in his early twenties ambled toward them. He was strongly built and muscled, with tattoos peeking from beneath the pushed-up sleeves of his hoodie. There was a mix of strength and caution in the way he moved. As he drew closer, Hope noticed his wary blue eyes under sandy-coloured, tousled hair.

"Sorry, mate," he said to Joe. "She doesn't know where her boundary lines are yet."

Joe nodded. "That's okay. When my lab, Bounty, moves out here with me, he'll probably just extend a permanent welcome mat."

Joe introduced Jesse to Hope. He offered a firm handshake.

"Are you new to the area, Jesse? I only moved into town last year myself," Hope said, offering a gentle smile, hoping to soften the guarded air around him.

Jesse shrugged. "Yep. I'm hoping to make a go of it out here with my Pop for a while. We're doing up his old farmhouse in case he needs to sell in the next couple of years."

"If you're handy with a hammer, Jesse, I might recruit you for some work over here," Joe said thoughtfully.

"I actually do need a paying job while I'm here. It'd be great if you know anyone who's looking for someone ..."

"We'll certainly keep a lookout for you," Hope said warmly.

Jesse nodded in thanks and headed back the way he'd come, whistling for Rusty to follow.

Something in his haunted eyes reminded Hope of Ruby when she'd first arrived at the café.

Joe watched Jesse disappear into the trees, his gaze thoughtful. "I hear he's recently spent some time in prison. Everyone's carrying something," he said quietly. "Sometimes all it takes is a neighbour and a second chance."

Hope watched him go, a quiet ache stirring at the memory of how she too had once needed someone to believe in her.

She then stepped closer, her eyes drifting from Jesse back to Joe.

"He'll be blessed to have you next door. Will you be moving here soon?"

"Yes. Ethan Betts, the new vet, arrives in a few months. He'll be taking over my cottage behind the surgery. Fresh start for both of us." He smiled. "He's young. Eager. Has no idea how stubborn the local dogs, and their owners, can be."

Hope laughed.

Joe's hand brushed the back of his neck. "There's something else." He pulled off his glove, then slowly, almost reverently, slid his wedding ring from his finger and slipped it into his coat pocket.

"I'll always love Anna," he said softly. "Loving her taught me how to give without holding on too tightly. I want to carry that forward, with honesty. And with you, if you'll let me."

He moved closer, voice low and steady.

"I'm not asking for promises or answers today. Just a beginning. A chance to see what God might grow between us."

Hope looked at him. She saw his humility and courage, and the open hands of a man who had suffered but was still offering love.

"I'm willing," she said quietly. "But I'm still healing, Joe."

He nodded. "Me too. Every day."

There was a long pause before she added, "But I'm not afraid—now—of seeing where we might go."

Joe smiled and opened his arms to her. She stepped into them.

And for a while, they stood in silence beneath the gum trees, where the cold no longer mattered, and the quiet held the promise of something new.

EPILOGUE

The wisteria in the café's backyard was in bloom, pale lavender petals tumbling over the wooden beams like something out of a storybook. The summer heat had softened into a golden afternoon, and laughter drifted across the yard from the tables where everyone had gathered for lunch.

Ruby sat beneath the jasmine-covered trellis, baby Samuel Thomas nestled in a cotton sling against her chest. Samuel, for the boy prophet who listened when God called. And Thomas, a quieter name, for the courage it takes to doubt and still keep going.

Hope appeared with a tall glass of homemade lemonade. She set it on the table with a smile.

"You two look good together," she said. "And ..." she nodded toward the new vet, Ethan, who was hovering nearby, pretending not to glance their way, "I don't think I'm the only one who's noticed that new-mum glow."

Ruby smiled but waved it off. "I certainly don't need more offers to hold him. You and Row between you have arms ready the moment I so much as blink."

Hope grinned. "We've got a good system."

"We've got a village," Ruby corrected softly, looking around at the timber tables, sprawled dogs, and shared food.

Hope's heart caught for a moment. There it was. The thing she used to think she'd missed. A life threaded with connection, built from second chances.

"We've both benefitted from Rowena's mother-wisdom," she said, watching as Row passed around slices of watermelon. "If it had been just you and me after Sam was born, it might've been a little … bumpier."

Ruby nodded. "She's been training the new mum, and the new grandma."

Hope stilled. A soft, uncertain laughter escaped her. "Still getting used to that one."

Ruby looked down at Sam's sleepy face. "You became it."

Hope blinked. "What?"

"I mean it." Ruby's voice had the quiet strength gained after hard things. "You didn't have to welcome me to stay. Or care. Or be what you are to me now. But you did. And you do."

Hope reached over, resting a hand lightly on Ruby's arm. "It's been the most unexpected blessing of my life."

Ruby smiled at her. "Mine too."

From across the garden, Rusty tore around the yard with Bounty and Asha close behind. Daisy stayed curled safely in Lily's arms, wide-eyed but curious.

Jesse walked over in his café apron, balancing a tray of drinks. He handed Ruby her hot chocolate, with oat milk, extra cinnamon. Exactly how she liked it.

"Thanks, Jesse," Ruby said, accepting it with a nod.

"Least I can do. You're keeping a whole person alive," he replied, not quite making eye contact.

They shared exchanges that had become routine, cordial, and careful. Jesse had been working part-time at the café for a few months now, trialling both the coffee machine and something closer to community.

He was still more shadow than sun, never one for lingering, but he showed up. On time. No attitude.

Still, Ruby kept her distance. Jesse was too good-looking to fully trust. And too quiet about his past. Word had spread, as it does in towns like Wombat Valley. People knew he'd been inside. Most didn't ask what for. But a few acted like they already knew.

Hope had vouched for him. And for now, that was enough.

They shared a brief moment of banter, still tentative, and still wrapped in the boundaries Ruby kept clear. Jesse had a past that cast long shadows. But he was trying. That counted.

Over near the garden bed, Lily handed Joe a drawing: him and Hope on a hill under a rainbow, two dogs and a baby in the distance. "That's for later," she told him with a grave nod.

Joe raised an eyebrow, grinning. "Is it now?"

Lunch had stretched long into the afternoon with lazy conversations and second helpings. As the sun began to dip, Joe stood and tapped his glass.

"I'll keep this short," he said. "But I need to say something."

The chatter faded. People turned to listen.

"Six months ago, I watched a woman step into the Wombat River and come up changed. Not by water, but by grace. I've seen her choose trust over fear, love over comfort. And I've learned something: love after loss isn't a replacement. It's resurrection. That's what Jesus does, He brings life where we thought only ashes remained."

He reached for Hope's hand.

"Yesterday, I asked Hope if she'd walk the rest of our seasons of life with me."

Hope stepped forward into his arms. Her smile was radiant, but steady.

"I said yes," she said simply.

They stood there, encircled by friends who had become family: Ruby and Samuel, Rowena, Nova and Lily, Tom and Eve, Edith and Rob, Dave and Rach, Hanna and Marcel, Mike and Suzanne, Craig, Jesse, and Ethan.

Hope's eyes landed on Ruby's across the crowd.

And in that glance, something deeper passed between them. It was more than gratitude, and more than love. A mutual knowing, forged in fire. Ruby gave a small nod, one arm curled around Samuel, her smile full of quiet joy.

Toward the back of the yard, Jesse leaned against the wall, sipping his coffee slowly.

When Joe spoke, about resurrection and grace, something shifted under Jesse's skin. Not longing, exactly.

Just … the ache of wondering.

Could someone like him fit in a world like this?

He looked away before anyone could notice the flicker in his eyes. The warmth of the afternoon felt both too much and not enough.

Joe turned back to Hope, reaching into his pocket. From it, he pulled a small velvet box.

Hope froze. Her breath caught.

Then, in front of their circle of witnesses, Joe knelt and asked her again.

He slipped the ring onto her finger. It was gold, patterned with an unbroken grape vine.

Hope looked into his eyes and saw a future of joyful mornings and shared love, where a cord of three strands woven together can't easily be broken.

***

Journal Entry – 15th January

> *God of new beginnings,*
> *Joe asked me to marry him.*
> *Not with grand gestures or a diamond chandelier. Just with gentle words, that were so sincere.*
> *And I said yes.*
> *Not because I've figured everything out.*
> *But because when he looks at me, I don't see my past. I see grace.*
> *You walked with me through ashes. Whispered truth into silence.*
> *And somehow, You've given me joy in life again. Not as a replacement, but as redemption.*
> *Thank You, Father God, for calling and waiting while I wandered. For never giving up, even when I couldn't pray.*
> *Thank You for Joe. For Ruby. For Samuel, and this messy, genuine community of Wombat Valley.*
> *The future still holds unknowns. But I'm not afraid anymore, because You are with me.*
> *May my story remind anyone in the valley: grace is always within reach.*
> *With You.*
>
> *Hope*

ACKNOWLEDGEMENTS
AND REFLECTIONS

Writing this novel about Hope Elkins, Joe Butler, and the cast of characters in Wombat Valley has been such a joy, and an incredible learning experience.

Hope's character and the women who surround her, were inspired by aspects of my own life story and by the lives of women I've walked alongside. Many of the characters' names are drawn from my own maternal family tree, reaching back seven generations.

While the novel explores painful experiences, it also allows the characters to grow in strength and wisdom. Writing it has been a deeply therapeutic journey for me, and I pray it offers healing to some readers, or insight for those walking alongside someone who is hurting.

The setting of Wombat Valley was inspired by the beautiful small village where I live on the NSW South Coast, and by nearby towns nestled in valleys along the coastal side of the Southern Highlands. Rural communities like these are places where kindness and connections can flourish.

I am profoundly grateful for the support and encouragement of my family throughout this writing journey. My husband, who comes from his own complex family background, has lovingly supported me every step of the way. He is rarely surprised by my ideas or the determined focus I bring once a plan takes shape.

This story has grown out of hundreds of hours of creative writing, prayerful reflection, and the help of some modern editing tools, including AI. Above all, I feel deeply privileged to have written a novel that does not point to ourselves as the source of hope, but to a Saviour who alone brings healing and restoration.

May the Spirit of God lead those who meet Him in these pages to open the Bible for themselves and discover that Jesus Christ holds all the words of hope we need.

Thank you to my family members and friends who read chapters or the whole manuscript, offering honest feedback, and words of encouragement along the way. Your input sharpened and strengthened this novel, and I'm deeply grateful.

I hope my daughter, stepdaughters, and granddaughter will one day meet and marry men with the compassion, kindness, strength of character, and wisdom of a man like Joe Butler.

I pray that my sons and grandson continue to grow into men who know that true strength is found in humility. May they love their wives and children well, support the vulnerable, and stand for truth. I hope they will be part of faith communities led by people who reflect the character of Jesus, like Tom and Eve.

And to you, dear reader, thank you. It is my prayer that this story blesses your life in a restorative way.

This movement into a genre of healing fiction, with characters who are broken but seeking community, lived faith, and real empathy, is something that God has laid on my heart.

There are more characters to introduce in Wombat Valley, and a growing ministry there to welcome others in. So don't be surprised if Hope and Joe return to share more of their story with you.

In love and grace,
Philippa

A NOTE TO CHURCH LEADERS

Dear Pastors, Church Elders, and Ministry Teams,

Thank you for taking the time to engage with individual chapters or the whole story of *Restoring Hope*. While this is a work of fiction, it reflects very real experiences faced by individuals in our churches, who are people navigating domestic violence, coercive control, betrayal, fear, and the struggle to find safety while holding onto their faith.

Sadly, the church has not always responded well to these situations. Whether through silence, minimisation, or misplaced theology, those suffering in harmful relationship situations have too often felt unseen, unheard, or spiritually misunderstood.

My hope is that this story might serve as a **conversation-starter**, for your leadership teams, small groups, or pastoral care ministries. How can we ensure that our churches are safe spaces for those living in fear? How can we walk with survivors in ways that uphold their dignity, affirm their agency, and reflect the heart of Christ?

Restoring Hope invites us to sit with the complexity of suffering, but also to imagine what restoration can look like when faith communities lead with wisdom, compassion, and moral courage. May it be a small part of a much-needed movement toward trauma-aware, spiritually grounded care in the Body of Christ.

With deep respect and hope,
Philippa

DISCUSSION GUIDES – RESTORING HOPE

The following Discussion Guides are available as free PDF downloads from the author's website **www.philippacleall.com**

- Discussion Guide for Church Leaders and Pastoral Carers - Confronting Abuse and Protecting Victims

- Discussion Questions for Book Club Groups

- Discussion Guide on The Trauma of Abuse and Challenge of Healing

- Discussion Guide Supporting Unplanned Pregnancy and Life Choices

www.ingramcontent.com/pod-product-compliance
Lightning Source LLC
Chambersburg PA
CBHW020832260626
47169CB00003B/942